LANDING PARTY

RICK CHESLER

SEVERED PRESS
HOBART TASMANIA

LANDING PARTY

Copyright © 2016 Rick Chesler
Copyright © 2016 Severed Press

WWW.SEVEREDPRESS.COM

ISBN: 978-1-925493-55-9

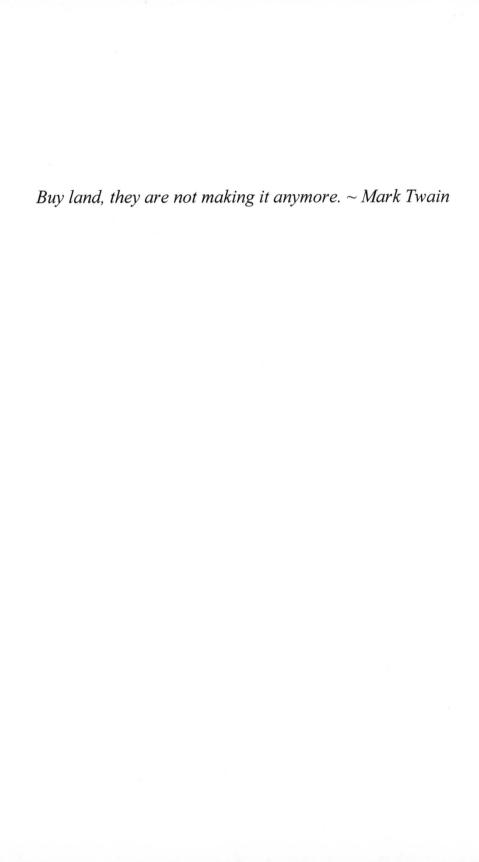

Buy land, they are not making it anymore. ~ Mark Twain

PROLOGUE

Present day, South Pacific Ocean

Atama Tokolahi stood on the deck of his old fishing boat, hauling in what he hoped would be the last net of the day. The catch hadn't been great so far, and as an elderly man, he recalled far better days, and indeed, far better years. There used to be more fish, he was sure of that. But things were what they were, and he didn't know how to do anything else, nor did he want to do anything else. He used to command a far larger operation, though, with three boats, each with a crew of half a dozen men. Now it was just him, alone on his simple wooden dory with its single, smoky engine. The market wouldn't bear more than that. The entire Tongan fishing fleet had shrunk over the decades, right along with the fish stocks.

Even so, he usually had what he needed, for himself and his extended family. They lived simply, in a hut by the shore, and they ate well. That was all he could ask for. But as he pulled the net into the boat, Atama could see he was coming up light, very light, and that he would need to do one more cast. Shaking his head as he removed the single tuna he'd caught, a "schoolie" size that more than twenty years ago would have been tossed back alive, Atama had resigned himself to preparing for one more throw of the net when he sensed something was not right.

He wasn't sure what it was at first. Just a vague sense of "differentness," or something about to happen. He wouldn't have been able to put it into words, but something made him look up and across the water. And there it was: smoke. Or was it ash? He squinted, eyes which had never known sunglasses focusing on the surface of the water perhaps a hundred yards distant. Then, much nearer to his small boat: the water began to smoke and bubble madly around him. His features took on a rare confused expression. He'd seen everything that could happen out here over the decades—freak weather, storms, strange animals, odd boats, weird people—what could this be?

Suddenly, a large mass was thrust above the surface of the water, and Atama moved to his outboard motor to put distance between his boat and whatever it was that came rising up out of the depths of the sea. Huge chunks of bright orange liquid spewed into the air as he turned his vessel around and put some space between himself and the disturbance. Curiosity got the better of him, though, and when he felt he was a safe distance away, he stopped to watch the spectacle unfold.

Massive plumes of fire skyrocketed from the water, and suddenly Atama knew.

Volcano!

He immediately knelt on the wet deck of his humble boat and prayed to the ancient Polynesian fire and volcano gods. He had seen active volcanoes erupt many times before, but on land, never one that emerged so suddenly from the sea. It was stunning, majestic, terrifying and unbelievable all at once.

As the orange liquid fire splashed down on the surface of the water, spitting off steam with angry hisses, the frothy lava turned brown and black as it cooled and solidified. More and more material was ejected from the bowels of the sea, piling on top of itself as a mystified Atama suddenly understood what he was witnessing: a new island was forming before his very eyes.

He watched the new land being born for a time, until his sense of self-preservation overcame his inquisitiveness, and he made the decision to head for port. He did not carry a camera, but he did mark the position of the natural spectacle with his GPS navigation device. Perhaps if he came back here some time later, it would be an excellent new fishing spot. He looked forward to letting his people know about this new land in their sacred territorial waters with which the spirits had blessed them.

One thing was for sure, though, as he watched the lava piling up. He wouldn't be getting any more fishing done today. But he had one heck of a story to tell.

CHAPTER 1

Two months later
United Nations Headquarters, New York City

"Ladies and gentlemen, we've been summoned here today because we have a problem developing in the South Pacific."

Hiroki Fujita, Secretary-General of the United Nations, looked at the stern faces of the twenty-two people gathered around the long, mahogany table. They had been called here for a special session of the United Nations Environment Programme, and they knew full well that any time they were called in for a sudden "special session," it was rarely good news or a simple situation. Today was no exception.

An image was projected on a wall screen and Fujita continued. "This is an aerial photograph taken from a U.S. National Oceanic and Atmospheric Administration reconnaissance flight, which took off from American Samoa after hearing reports of unusual volcanic activity in the region."

A chorus of exclamations and low whistles erupted around the table as they took in the sight of a conical mountain rising from the blue ocean. Fujita waited for the hubbub to die down and went on. "You're looking at the newest land planet Earth has to offer. This is a brand new island that formed as a result of undersea volcanic activity. It first broke the ocean surface only two months ago, and has since solidified to the point it has become an actual land mass."

"Does it have a name?" This from one of the younger attendees, a recent Ivy League political science graduate.

"Officially, it is not yet named, although four neighboring island nations have each given it a name in their respective native language. The Tongans are calling it, *Hunga Tonga- Ha'apai,* which translates loosely into English as "sacred place of nurturing fire."

A short, squat, swarthy woman wearing spectacles posed a question some of the others had on their minds. "So what's the problem? Was this eruption only the tip of the iceberg? Is the region under threat from additional volcanic activity?"

Fujita shook his head. "To the contrary, by all indications, it seems to have stabilized except for highly localized activity continuing on the new island itself. But the wider region is under no particular threat to life or property."

The delegate lifted her hands in a questioning gesture. "So if there is no threat, then why are we here?"

A smattering of hushed conjecture quickly evaporated as Fujita responded. "The problem is that the island nation of Tonga sent a landing party to claim ownership by being first to land and plant a flag. However, that party has not been heard from since being dispatched a week ago. Meanwhile, the neighboring nations, including the Cook Islands, Niue, and Western Samoa, claim that the disappearance is a trick or stunt of some kind, that in fact the Tonga landing party members are still alive and well on the island."

"Why would they hide?" a rail-thin Israeli man asked.

Fujita responded while clicking a remote control to advance the slide. "Allegations—as yet unfounded—are that the Tongans are building a defense installation in secret."

The next image showed a closer view of the island's steep, rocky sides, shrouded in vapors. "It does not appear to have a lot of flat ground suitable for such purposes, but as you can see, it is difficult to make out much detail from these photographs. He clicked through a couple more, showing the island from different angles but about the same distance away. Heavy vapor cover in every picture made it hard to discern much detail.

"That is why," he said, putting down the remote, "we are going to assemble an expedition to go in as a neutral party and assess the situation. It will be formally designated as the Gaia Expedition, 'Gaia' referring to the Greek goddess who gave birth to the Earth. Among its goals will be to evaluate whether the land is, in fact, habitable, for one thing—is it even worth fighting over? For another, to determine the fate of the Tongan landing party and to report to the world on that fate. If military activity is discovered, we are only to observe and document it. Our representatives will not be armed beyond conventional field tools such as utility knives and axes. Again, we are there only to report and document what is happening as a neutral party."

An aide spoke in a low voice into Fujita's ear, and the U.N. leader perked up, nodding. He then added, "That being said, we have been green lighted for a special contingency option."

"Green lighted by whom?" a representative from India inquired.

"In coordination with the United States military operating out of American Samoa, we have a 'code red' option available to us." He paused to look around the table. Seeing that he had the undivided attention of everyone in the room, Fujita went on. "In order to prevent future conflict from escalating into possible warfare, *or* if the island itself is so unstable that it poses a hazard to nearby countries, we are authorized to bomb the island sufficiently to destabilize it until it is no longer a coherent, contiguous land mass."

Surprised murmurs made their way around the table.

"This is only as an extreme measure in the face of unforeseen circumstances. Based on what we know so far, it is highly doubtful it will need to be utilized, but our expedition members will be made aware of the option nonetheless. Which brings us to our next matter of discussion," Fujita added. "The expedition team itself."

"How many people on our expedition?" This from a long-time Japanese delegate.

Fujita nodded, glad that the topic of conversation was moving on from the explosive option. "Eight well-chosen individuals should offer sufficient expertise and presence."

"Who are they?" This from a Venezuelan representative.

Fujita took a deep breath. "We have a large pool of prospective participants to sort through." He nodded to an assistant who pressed keys on a laptop computer.

"Let's get to work and figure out who the lucky ones will be, shall we?"

CHAPTER 2

Nuku'alofa, Tonga

CIA Special Agent Valea Esau got off the public bus in the bustling downtown section of the capital city. His nearest formal base of operation was the American embassy in Suva, Fiji, which covered a large swath of the South Pacific, but he'd been living in Tonga for two years. The locals knew him as an auto mechanic. That was his job and how he supported himself, for he had no family. A single Pacific Islander who had fun when he wasn't working—fishing, scuba diving, frequenting the local bars. No one thought anything of it.

Valea stopped while he pretended to study the bus stop sign, his peripheral vision highly active behind his polarized sunglasses. Satisfied he had not been followed, he began walking into the city. He moved at a quick pace, but not so fast as to attract attention. This was not New York City, and the pace of life in the South Pacific was generally a little slower. After nearly an hour of walking, due to a circuitous route which involved numerous stops to confirm he was still not being tracked, Valea came to the Royal Palace of Tonga.

A red and white wooden building constructed in the 1800s, it was one of many homes sometimes occupied by the king, although Valea knew the Tongan ruler would be here today. He reached the gate and was greeted by two guards wearing starched and pressed white uniforms. He stated his name and that he had an appointment, and one of the guards escorted Valea into the palace.

The building was sparsely populated for a place of political leadership, and Valea saw few people as he was led up broad stairs to the second floor of the residence. From there, they went down a long, wood-floored hallway to a closed door at the end of the hall. The guard knocked once and heard a female voice tell him to open the door. He led Valea inside where the receptionist informed Valea that King Malo Nau was ready to see him. A young, pretty woman, she made lingering eye contact with Valea, who did his best to return it just long enough to be polite as he entered the king's private suite while the guard remained in the reception area.

"Good afternoon, Esau, I trust you are doing well?" A corpulent man in his early sixties, the king's beard and mustache were white, even though his curly hair was still dark. Valea had never garnered the courage to ask him if he dyed his hair. In public, the king wore fancy robes and regalia, but today, as usual when he remained in the palace, he wore a casual resort-style outfit of linen shirt and pants, with leather sandals.

"Personally, Your Majesty, I am doing fine, thank you. But you know I do not request a meeting with you—"

"Unless a situation is brewing, yes, of that I am well aware." King Nau moved to a wet bar and waved a hand over an array of crystal decanters. "No matter how pressing our business may be, there is always time to be civilized. Would you care for some fine rum?"

Esau accepted, knowing he was technically in the line of duty as an agent of the United States working on foreign soil, but at the same time aware that fostering good diplomatic relations was a key part of his job. The king passed him a squat, crystal glass, and the two men moved to two plush chairs arranged around a coffee table that looked as though it was made of ivory.

"Now tell me, Valea, what is it that's on your mind? Be frank with me, be honest." The king's eyes bored into Valea's over their drinks.

"It's about the new island, Your Majesty."

The king nodded. "Like new nations—of which Tonga is one—as you know we only fully gained independence from the British in 1970—new islands take time; they are born of fire and slowly cool into something that is usable and hospitable. So what about *Hunga Tonga- Ha'apai*? What worries you?"

Valea took another sip of his drink and then set it down on the table in order to fully focus his response. "Your Majesty, as you know, the landing party you sent to the island has failed to return."

The king shrugged. "How do we know they are not still there?"

Valea appeared doubtful, throwing his hands up. "Satellite photos and recon flyovers disguised as weather patrols show no sign of them. Their mission was to establish a Tongan presence and make that presence known to the world so that this island would be indisputably part of Tonga."

The king's eyes narrowed somewhat. "*Hunga Tonga- Ha'apai* is very much a part of Tonga. The newest part!" He smiled as he said the last sentence.

But Valea did not share in the mirth. "Not everyone will call the island what you have named it, Your Majesty. The Samoans already have their own name, as does Niue and the Cook Islands. Without an uncontested Tongan presence…"

"Yes, yes, the Americans will not be able to make use of the new island for their military operations. That is your fear, is it not?"

"You know who I work for, Malo. What our agreement entails. For your country to receive the promised revenue stream for our base to be allowed to operate on the new island, in secrecy, then you first must establish clear, uncontested ownership of said island."

"I sent a landing party!"

"I know you did, Malo, but they failed to return. So it is time for next steps. That is why I come before you today."

"What are you saying, that I did not honor my side of the deal?" The king stood, eyes flashing.

"Please, Your Majesty. Be seated. I am only trying to get you the revenue stream you said you desired, and which, I might add," Valea said, glancing toward the window, "your country badly needs. Fishing stocks are down, your country has no real industry to speak of other than light tourism. We offer you real revenue so that you won't have to try the crazy things that have failed for you in the past. Remember when you proposed making part of Tonga a disposal site for nuclear waste?"

The king flushed, apparently embarrassed. "That was an offhand remark about one of our outlying atolls—*one* of them out of hundreds. It was never a formal proposal. Now listen: I sent a landing party when you asked! You have to uphold your side of the deal as well!"

"As you know, King Nau, we created the earthquake that caused the volcanic eruption."

"Yes, Project...what was it you called it? Neptune's Inferno!" He smiled as if this was highly entertaining to him.

"Yes, but now there has been a new development, and I am here to inform you of it."

The king sat and finished the rest of his drink. "Go ahead, I am listening."

"Unfortunately, the United Nations is sending in a well-outfitted expedition consisting of seasoned explorers and scientists to land on the island and determine the fate of your landing party."

The king shrugged and started to say something, but Valea cut him off. "If they determine that there is no Tongan presence on the island, it could open the land up to colonization by the neighboring countries I mentioned earlier."

"Yes, and that worries you because the U.S. does not have deals with those countries, am I right?"

"That is correct, Malo. Our deal was with you, because our analysts determined a better-than-average probability that Tonga would be able to lay claim to the island. But things haven't gone smoothly."

"So what are you proposing? What do you want me to do?"

Valea spread his hands out in a soothing gesture. "You need only to listen and play along. No real action will be required on your part."

"Explain." The king leaned forward.

"We—the CIA—have placed a mole in the U.N. expedition."

"You mean, a *spy*?" The king's eyes widened, as though he were excited like a kid watching an espionage movie.

Valea made a disapproving expression. "We prefer the term *asset*. He's just a guy who's on our side, Malo, who has instructions to make it look like Tonga got to the island first. In the event that..." Valea hesitated as if unsure of how to explain what was on his mind.

"In the event that *what*?"

"In the event that none of your landing party ever made it to the island in the first place."

King Nau's eyes bulged, and a vein stood out on his temple. "What? Are you accusing me of not sending the landing party?"

Valea shook his head rapidly. "No, no, no, of course not."

9

"Well, then what are you insinuating?"

Valea took a deep breath. "It's possible they never made it to the island, Malo. There was a squall shortly after they left, they could have been blown off course, adrift, sunk…"

King Nau threw his head back and laughed heartily. "That is what you are worried about? That my Tongan sailors—men who come from a long line of seafarers in an oceanic nation—managed not to reach a location only a day's sail away? One that was reported to me in the first place by our own local fishermen?"

"It's a possibility we can't afford to overlook, Malo, that's all I'm saying. That's why we went through the trouble to place a mole on the U.N.'s expedition."

Nau shrugged. "All right. I could send another landing party…"

"No. That would appear overly aggressive and could make things more difficult. Part of the reason the U.N. is involved is as a peacekeeper. The spat over ownership of the new island has been making international headlines. You already had a shot at it. Another one would be perceived as…"

"Okay, I get it. So you think that your man on this expedition can…do what?"

"He can make it look like your party got there first, Malo, even if they didn't. All I need for you to do is to confirm it—don't act surprised if and when you're asked about it by the media—and don't provide any details without consulting with me first. Understand?"

"And our deal stands as before, correct?"

Valea nodded. "It does."

King Nau smiled and got up. "Then I understand. I will refresh our drinks."

CHAPTER 3

Two days later
Montreal, Canada

Skylar Hanson wasn't sure when the idea first came to her, only that it was a good one. Well, perhaps "good" wasn't the right word. It was the "right" one, and she was content to leave it at that. As a volcanologist for the Canadian government, Skylar studied volcanoes for a living. Earning a Ph.D. at the age of 25 meant that she had been an academic star, had done an awful lot of reading about geological processes and how the Earth was and continues to be formed.

And somewhere along the way, those same processes came to shape how she was formed, as well. Skylar, at the age of thirty-three, was aware that though she was a respected member of society, one who would likely never want for a job and therefore be financially secure the rest of her natural life as long as she didn't do anything really foolhardy, she was still not truly happy. All she did was work, for one thing. Day in and day out, unraveling the mysteries of the Earth's innermost workings in order to explain them to policymakers—people who, for the most part, made a lot more money than she did—yet who she saw as much less intelligent.

Skylar was relatively young to reach such a jaded outlook, but then again, she'd always been ahead of the curve, skipping a grade in school and flying through one honors class to the next, shrugging them off like water off the proverbial duck's back. Good going, kid, keep it up, was all she ever heard. Now, only eight years of full-time employment into her professional career, she'd decided she'd had enough...or at least, that she *knew* enough.

Knew enough to get out of it, that is.

A thin smile formed on Skylar's lips as she eyeballed the aerial photographs of a new volcanic island forming in the South Pacific. The photos were taken by NOAA and not yet made public; she had received them because they came as part of an invitation from the United Nations to participate in an expedition to the newly formed island. She couldn't fault them in their choice to reach out to her. She was one of probably a dozen people on the planet best suited to characterize what was going on with the geological forces at work to create this new land.

But what they couldn't know was that the more she studied the island, the more she came to be convinced that she had before her a once in a lifetime opportunity—a perfect storm of physical, political, and financial factors that would never be presented to her again. She was ready to make a move, but first, she had to be sure.

Skylar got up from her laptop and moved to a floor-to-ceiling bookshelf overflowing with volumes, all of them non-fiction, including every textbook she'd ever had throughout her scholastic career. She had no need for fiction, no time for anything that was not wholly real and could tell her how the natural world worked. She found the shelf she had created with books about gemstones and the physical and chemical processes that create them.

Sometime later, she moved to another shelf with tome after tome written on volcanic processes. She knew what she was looking for, and it didn't take long for her to find. Unlike most of her peers in her generation, when it came to her areas of expertise, she rarely needed the internet, preferring instead to consult books, many of which were written decades before she was born. In geological terms, after all, that was not even the blink of an eye, so how much could things have changed? She secretly looked down on her colleagues who clung to the internet like it was the only bastion of reliable information out there, reading each new journal article the second it came out. Skylar knew how to do that, had jumped through every hoop put in front of her during her ascent to becoming a professional scientist, but she was so very sick of it all.

She knew enough already, enough to…what was that old American country song? *Take This Job and Shove It.*

Skylar went back to her laptop and reread the email from the U.N. again, the part with the description of the new island. It was cobbled together from Pacific Islander eyewitnesses and meteorologists, therefore a laypersons' account, but it was nevertheless sufficient for Dr. Skylar Hanson to conclude that there must be gemstone inclusions in this new land. Lots of them. Diamonds in particular. She closed the email window and called up the images of the new isle again.

Yes...definitely...there can be no doubt... But this certainty raised new concerns, new fears. There had already been one landing party. It wouldn't be long before others made landfall, too, each seeking to make their own mark on the island in some way. And even Skylar's own opportunity to visit Earth's newest waterfront property was as part of a group—an entire expedition under the auspices of the U.N. for the purposes of keeping the peace.

Her eyes narrowed as she stared a picture of an active lava flow, the ocean waves exploding around it. Even worse than being part of an eight-person team was that one of the other members would also be a geologist. Skylar closed out of the image. She'd done enough research. She knew all she needed to about the island. As far as she could tell from this distance, it should be positively chock full of precious gems, especially diamonds.

The only thing that remained was her decision. Was she going to go? She briefly entertained various alternatives to participating in the official expedition while still allowing her to make off with a pile of diamonds.

She could charter a private seaplane, she supposed, from Samoa or Tonga and ask to be taken to the island by herself. But that would no doubt raise too many suspicions. Especially in light of the fact that she recently turned down an invitation to join the U.N. expedition. No, way too many questions would come out of that. But if she were to join the expedition and take home a few souvenirs... Diamonds didn't have to be very big to be worth an awful lot, after all...

Couldn't she just pocket a few stones and come home wealthy, quietly leave her government post and retire somewhere warm and tropical instead of being snow and ice-bound for the rest of her life? Skylar grinned as her gaze lingered on a book open to an illustration of diamonds forming deep within the Earth...

Sure, you can. Those diamonds will be there, waiting for you. You just have to go get them. You've studied them all your life, they're yours...take them...

But then what? How would she sell a bunch of raw, uncut gemstones? She thought back to various field locations she'd worked at over the years, all the way back to her undergraduate days. She could think of at least a couple of places, far from her home, where there wouldn't be too many questions asked. Besides, she mused, opening the U.N. email to reply in the affirmative, it wasn't like she was stealing them from a jewelry store or anything like that. She would simply be collecting rocks out of the Earth—land as yet unaffiliated with any nation, at that—and then trading them for money.

It would represent professional suicide, no doubt. A scientist being paid to investigate a site as part of a sponsored, neutral organization would be prohibited from harvesting any sort of natural resources from that place for personal gain. But at the same time, Skylar knew she would have a lot of leeway. No one would have any reason to watch her closely, and it was perfectly within her bounds to collect a small amount of samples to bring back for laboratory study…

She nodded to herself, her resolve hardened as she composed the email that would make her a part of U.N. Expedition Gaia.

#

London, England

Richard Eavesley used a cigar cutter to snip the end off a Cuban, then applied the flame of his gold-plated butane lighter to the tip. He inhaled and puffed until smoke wafted from the tip, and then sat back in the leather upholstered chair to wait. He set the cutter and lighter on a small table next to a perfectly crafted mojito. He'd just returned from an "expedition" of sorts to Cuba, sponsored by a travel company with the goal of identifying the most travel-ready destinations and "adventure" ready packages for American tourists, now that Cuban-American relations had finally relaxed some.

The trip was a lucrative one for Eavesley, to be sure, but he would be the first to admit it was not the stuff of true adventure, the life-and-death derring-do that had made him a member of the prestigious British Explorers Club, not to mention a National Geographic Explorer-In-Residence, in the first place.

Richard looked around at the club, at the ornate furnishings, the taxidermy trophies on the wall, the old photographs of white men in foreign lands, killing animals, fording streams, driving vintage jeeps over rough terrain. A massive, old wooden canoe built by Amazon tribesmen hung from the ceiling. As usual, the club was not crowded, being a strict members-only affair. A few others from his recent Cuba trip were here, also celebrating a successful outing, sharing anecdotes over a laugh and a drink. This was an old boys' network, with Richard one of its most entrenched members. But while most of those here were discussing the Cuban trip or fantasizing about future adventures, Richard's thoughts wandered to a proposition he'd received earlier in the day. He'd come here curious to see if everyone would be talking about it—if the entire club had been invited—but from the utter lack of talk, it seemed he was the only one, which of course made it all the more interesting.

A real adventure. That's how he thought of it—one of those rare, larger-than-life explorations that would stand out in a career full of globe-spanning voyages of discovery. He hadn't responded yet—the email had just come in over his smartphone, and he didn't want to seem too eager, but he intended to apply in the affirmative as soon as he got home from the club. By the time he had polished off most of his drink and engaged in a little more small talk with the other members, he was preparing to leave when a well-dressed gentleman Richard had never seen before pulled up a chair and engaged him in conversation.

Being an exclusive club, it was a rare enough thing for Richard not to recognize someone here, as he'd been a member for decades. So it was with genuine interest that he listened to what the man had to say.

"Afternoon, Mr. Eavesley. Sir Eavesley, in due time, I expect, yes?"

Richard laughed good-naturedly at the reference to someday being knighted for his service to the Queen in exploring new lands. "Time will tell, Mr....?"

The man extended a hand that protruded from a silk jacket sleeve decorated with gold cuff links. A matching gold Rolex watch adorned his wrist. "Just call me Baxter, Mr. Eavesley."

A bemused look occupied Richard's countenance. "All right, Baxter. Is that your first name or your last?"

"It really doesn't matter. You mind?" The visitor plucked a cigar from the table, cut it, and lit it up using his own lighter.

"Be my guest… Speaking of which, I don't believe I've seen you here before. Are you a new member?"

Baxter smiled easily. "I'm not a member, Mr. Eavesley."

"Ah, so then whose guest are you?" Richard looked around as if he would be able to spot someone lurking nearby, perhaps about to join the conversation, but there was no one in the immediate vicinity.

"I'm not a guest either, Richard."

Richard guffawed loudly, emitting a cloud of bluish smoke. "Oh really, then? So you just waltzed in here past the security guards? Or—no, let me guess—you scaled the brick wall to the fourth floor here and used a torch on the wrought iron bars. Do tell, if that is how you got in, I'd buy you a drink myself, that would be quite impress—"

"This is what got me through the door, Richard." Baxter held up a member ID, the club's coat of arms with Baxter's picture. The words NOVICE EXPLORER were stamped beneath his picture, a designation meaning he'd been a member for less than one year. Richard's own ID read ULTIMATE ADVENTURER.

"I thought you said you weren't a member?"

Baxter produced a different credential, this one bearing the seal of the American Central Intelligence Agency. "I'm not. I'm a case officer with the CIA, Mr. Eavesley, and I'd like to talk to you about the offer you received this morning to join the United Nations Expedition Gaia. Hear me out, and I assure you that I'll make it worth your while."

CHAPTER 4

Four days later
South Pacific Ocean

A never-ending expanse of blue water gave way to a blemish, a pimple on the face of the ocean. The eight members of the U.N. expedition occupied the rear seats of the Bell 412 helicopter as the pilot, a retired U.S. Navy aviator hired as a contractor by the U.N. for this expedition, pointed out of his window.

"There's your first look."

Their gazes followed the trail of smoke—light and wispy at this altitude—down to the open volcano from which it vented. One of the team's two geologists, a 37-year-old South African by the name of George Meyer, was the first to comment after an appreciable silence. His red hair and freckles with a high forehead that seemed to be perpetually sweaty gave him a nerdy, academic look.

"Classic cinder cone formation." He quickly pulled a pair of binoculars that hung around his neck up to his eyes, focused the lenses, and continued his commentary. "Looks like a slope of between thirty to forty degrees. Bowl-shaped crater at the peak." He spoke to everyone but his eyes focused on the expedition's only other scientist, 33-year-old Canadian, Skylar Hanson, also a geologist. In stark contrast to her fellow geologist, Skylar was used to lingering stares from the opposite sex. A brunette with shoulder-length, stylishly cropped hair, her trim figure was testament to her regular workout routine. She nodded without taking her eyes off of the volcano.

"I can't wait to collect some cinder samples and analyze the gas bubbles."

George nodded at this. "Top notch idea." While they were both geologists by training, he at Oxford because he had studied abroad there and she at the University of Toronto, George specialized in mining and land stability while Skylar was a volcanologist, specializing in volcanoes.

Skylar went on while the rest of the team stared out the window at the forbidding landscape that awaited them below. "Also, I'd really like to get a look at the crater infill." She leaned forward to address the pilot. "Is it safe to do a flyover of the summit so we can look down into it?"

He nodded while leaning back in the cockpit. "Sure, we can drop down a little lower and zip across. Not too much lower, though. Tricky updrafts, and this thing hasn't settled down completely by the looks of it, but you're the expert."

"I agree, not too low!"

The pilot leveled out the craft and aimed for the center of the summit on a course that would take them about five hundred feet over the peak. As they neared the oceanic mountain, rivers of orange could be seen coursing through parts of its rock mantle. One man clicked away furiously with a camera aimed out the window.

Ethan Jones, the expedition's official "imaging expert," was a 35-year-old Australian who was a renowned nature photographer. A head of thick, dark curly hair framed a pair of sea green eyes.

"Getting some good aerials, Ethan?" the pilot asked.

He gave him a thumbs up in return without removing his eye from the lens. "Awesome shots, mate! You fly, I'll spy!"

This elicited a chuckle from Richard Eavesley, one of the team's two professional explorers, both National Geographic Explorers-In-Residence. Dubbed the expedition's "elder statesman," a light-hearted nod to his 52 years of age, Richard hailed from England, though his round-the-world travels kept him away from home much of the time. By far the most seasoned explorer of the bunch, he was noted for having summited the highest peak on all seven continents. His thinning, white hair was confined to the sides of his head, but even so, his facial features still somehow imparted a youthful look to him.

"Those aerials might come in handy later when it comes to finding our way around. Not like there's any charts of this place yet, am I right?"

The first to answer him was the youngest member of the outfit, 29-year-old Lara Cantrel. As the expedition's Communications Technician and an M.I.T. grad from Connecticut, Lara was the most technically savvy of the group. She kept her sandy blonde hair in a ponytail that stuck through the back of a ball cap. "I'm taking GPS points as well, so that we'll be able to map accurate distances once we're on the ground by overlaying my points on Ethan's photos."

The photographer looked away from his camera, a devilish grin overtaking his features. "Sweetheart, you can overlay your points on my photo anytime, all right?" He gave an exaggerated wink along with a good-natured laugh and turned back to his image capturing. Lara rolled her eyes, but couldn't help but smile.

"Go ahead and smack him, I would." Richard's counterpoint, the other National Geographic Explorer-In-residence, one Anita Clarkson of California, weighed in. At 31 years old, she was an accomplished blue water sailor and most noted for being the youngest female to sail solo around the globe, at age sixteen. Her sky blue eyes hid behind disheveled, blonde bangs. Though she was Richard's peer, that didn't necessarily endear her to him.

"Remind me again what your expertise is, dear? I get that if we were sailing to the island your skills would come in handy, but seeing as we flew here..."

Anita shot him a look to kill. "We both have the same sponsor, Richard. The same people who deemed you suitable for the expedition felt the same way about me. So get over it."

A peanut gallery of "ooohs" echoed throughout the cabin as the helicopter approached the mouth of the volcano. Joystna Chandahar, a 39-year-old Indian-American and the team's medical doctor, raised her voice above the fray. She was all of four-foot-eleven inches, but her diminutive stature belied her quiet intensity. She wore her long, black hair parted in the middle, pausing often to sweep it back from her face, as she did now.

"C'mon, people, we've got to work together. I figured I would be here to help with field injuries, not cat-fights." Joystna possessed extensive experience in providing emergency aid in disaster-affected areas including India and Southeast Asia. She generally put out a serious demeanor and was not much for small talk.

"Okay, everybody. Here we are—take a look down there!" Kai Nguyen, the team's foreign language translator, pointed excitedly. A 42-year-old born in Hawaii but now living in Washington, D.C., Kai was brought into the fold because he was an expert on Pacific island languages. If the team did manage to locate any of the Tongan landing party still alive, they would need to communicate. Kai's wavy black hair and classic Polynesian features made him look more at home in this part of the world than the rest of the team, but the truth was that while he spent his childhood in Hawaii, he now passed most of his time in D.C., where many of his translation jobs were conducted via video chat, Internet or telephone. This was his first trip to the South Pacific in many years.

The craft flew directly over the middle of the volcano's peak, and those on either side of the helo looked directly down into it.

"There's a lake!" George pointed but the gesture was wholly unnecessary since it was easy to see that the entire bottom portion of the volcano was flooded with water.

"Seawater coming up from below or perhaps trapped inside during formation. Will be interesting to find out," Skylar said.

"What's not so interesting about it," Richard pointed out, "is that it means there's nowhere flat for us to put down in there."

At this, the pilot nodded. "After we fly across, we'll circle the perimeter and see if we can find a level enough spot there."

No one disagreed, and they flew over the yawning opening in silence. When they were about halfway across, Lara pointed excitedly.

"Look! I see something, something orange." She raised binoculars to her eyes and focused. "Looks like it could be a life jacket."

Ethan clicked off a few photos. "Definitely a good place to start looking, then."

When they reached the other side, the pilot made a right turn and began following the curve of the island's roughly circular form.

"Not a whole lot of optimal landing spots here, either. Maybe we should have come by boat after all." Anita glared at Richard, who shrugged as he looked down at the rugged new landscape.

"We'll see. We have yet to go all the way around."

But as the circumnavigation of the island continued, it became clear that the topography varied little. Steep, rocky sides thrust up from the open ocean with very few exceptions, and none of those were sufficient to land a helicopter. By the time they had gone all the way around, a sullen silence had fallen over the cabin as they all pondered the unspoken question: where to land?

At length, that silence was broken by Richard, the explorer who had figured out many a route into inhospitable places over the decades. "Look, the Tongans must have found a way either inside it or up onto it, right? And they came by boat..."

Anita, the sailor, was quick to reply. "Unless their boat sank on the way there—who knows, maybe they never even got here. There hasn't been any proof one way or the other."

The pilot interrupted them by leaning back and saying, "It's up to you, but we do have options. Let me lay them out. One: we can fly around a little more to try and find a nice flat landing zone, but when I reach my low fuel point, we'll have to head back to Samoa." He continued on over the groans in response. "Two: we can abort now and head back after seeing the place up close."

"Anything else?" Richard asked.

"Yeah, or three: We can try having Steve, here, lower you down wherever you want to go by winched cable." He patted his co-pilot on the shoulder, and Steve nodded.

"Then we'd pick you up the same way in reverse—lower it down, you grab hold of the basket, and I reel you back in."

"Just remember to ground ourselves first before we touch the cable, right, or zap!" Richard mimicked convulsions induced by electrocution.

The co-pilot grinned. "I see you've done this before."

Richard nodded. "More than once, I'm afraid. Somehow, it's always worked out for me so far."

"Let's hope that luck holds out, because I think at this point that's our best option."

"So where to lower us down?"

"All business as usual, eh, Dr. Chandahar?" Richard smiled in her direction. "I like it. I say we split up, if it's okay with our good pilot."

The pilot's brow furrowed. "Split up how? I don't have all day." He tapped his fuel gauge.

Richard was quick to reply, as he could see others about to protest as well. "Two groups of four. One dropped somewhere up on the outside slope, wherever you think you can pull it off. And the other to be dropped along with the inflatable boat down into the lake, near where we spotted that life jacket or whatever it is. That'll give us a chance to cover the most ground possible. This is considered a search-and-rescue mission, let's not forget. We should cover as much area as we possibly can."

The pilot pointed up and to the right. "Let's check out the outer slope up near the top. This side looked a little better to me, and then from there, we can drop in for the lake shot."

No one voiced an argument, although there were no actual agreements, either. Everyone still mulled over the ramifications of the plan, which had them suddenly from a comfortable helicopter ride to confronting the reality that they were going to *get out of the aircraft* and step onto a highly active volcano. This was not some inviting tropical island with a sugary sand beach and palm trees swaying in the breeze. There was no way to walk onto the isle at all. Or off of it.

The pilot ascended, and the team watched the pastiche of brown lava rock stripe vertically past their window, where spotty patches of molten lava bubbled up every so often. George pointed out the first traces of new plant life, already taking root in the rocky substrate, eking out a living on this harsh terrain.

They were jolted from their thoughts by the pilot waving to get their attention. "I can't land here, but I can hover a few feet off the ground until you can jump out."

"I'm game." Richard raised his hand like an eager school kid.

"Same here, mate." Ethan was grinning ear to ear, like this was the best thing he could possibly be doing.

A couple of seconds ticked by during which the noise of the rotors holding their position over the scorched ground was the only sound. "C'mon, who's next?"

Anita raised her hand and Richard frowned. "Really, dear, don't you think you ought to be on the boat team so we can at least make use of the narrow range of experience you do have?"

"Perhaps you should try the boat, Richard. Get out of your mountain climbing comfort zone."

"Enough!" Joystna, the M.D., raised her voice to a sharp trill, silencing the team. "I would have thought that the team's two professional explorers, both from the same organization no less, would at least have a working rapport."

"I don't mind being on the boat team," Anita offered.

George Meyer nodded. "If we're splitting up, we should probably split the expertise as well. We have two professional explorers, so one on each team." He looked at Skylar. "Two geologists, so one on each team." Skylar was quick to nod her agreement to this.

"Make sure we split up the sat-phones, as well," Kai suggested. Every member of the team carried a two-way radio, which would keep them in touch with each other over short distances on the island, but for contact with the outside world, only satellite phones would do. The team had two of them, so it was decided that one would go to each sub-team.

The group was in agreement, and they quickly worked out a roster for each team, designated Slope and Boat. By the time they had finished with that, the pilot was hovering over the Slope Team drop zone.

"This is as good as it's going to get for the slope. Looks like you have a little bit of semi- flat ground to get started on. After that, good luck!"

The helicopter descended to three feet above a rare level patch of ground and the four Slope Team members, each wearing a backpack, lined up to jump out. Richard Eavesley led the way, followed by geologist George Meyer, photographer Ethan Jones, and translator Kai Nguyen. The crunch of lava rock under boots was drowned out by the helicopter's engine. After all four duck-walked out from beneath the rotors, the chopper lifted off while the team still on board waved their temporary goodbyes.

The pilot lifted the craft higher and then moved forward until they cleared the lip of the volcano. In the back, Anita and Skylar worked to unpack their small inflatable raft. It would float the four of them and their gear, but just barely. As they inflated it with a hand pump, they stuck the nose out the door. Meanwhile, the craft descended, and it became noticeably darker inside the volcano, light only penetrating from directly above.

"Anybody notice something funny?" Anita asked the group, her blonde eyebrows furrowing above sky blue eyes.

"What's that?" Skylar didn't look up from adjusting the straps on her backpack.

"We split the two teams into men and women."

All four women of the Boat Team looked around at one another and burst out laughing. "Probably better that way, no distractions, right?" Lara said.

"On my go, people…" The pilot's voice put an end to their banter. His hand moved over the controls as he steadied the aircraft a few feet above the lake's surface, now whipped into a frenzy of whitewater by the rotor wash.

Anita grabbed hold of a rope tied to the raft. They had fastened a weight to the nose of the raft to make sure it would drop down and not get buffeted into the rotors, destroying their boat and possibly the helicopter, too.

"Here goes." She and Skylar kicked the little boat out the door.

Even with the added ballast, the lightweight raft caught an updraft, and for one heart-stopping moment, it seemed the raft was going to hit the rotors, but then it slanted down at an angle and hit the water. Their luck wasn't perfect, however, since it landed upside-down.

Anita cursed the turn of events. She still held the rope attached to the raft, keeping it from being blown across the lake by the rotor wash.

"Now what?" Joystna asked. "Haul it back up and try again?"

It was the helicopter pilot who answered. "No way. That was too close to the rotors. We're not trying that again. Deal with it. Get down there and flip it over."

Before anyone could say anything, Anita jumped out the door, splashing into the lake a few feet from the boat. Those in the helo looked down on her, waiting to see she if was okay. What if the water was still almost boiling hot? They'd all heard the predictions, based on science—it should be about the same as the surrounding ocean water, maybe a little warmer—but still. Here she was, actually taking the plunge. Another unsettling thought—what if the water wasn't that deep and she hit the bottom hard?

But Anita gave a casual wave to let them know she was okay after making the drop. Then, using the rope, she pulled the raft to her. It was light enough that she was able to flip it over herself. She did so and then shrugged off her pack. She chucked it up and over, into the raft. Then she got in herself, kicking until she was able to flop inside.

Skylar Hanson was next to jump, followed quickly by Joystna Chandahar and Lara Cantrel. The chopper rose up and out of the volcano as soon as all of the passengers were clear, lessening the rotor wash for the swimmers. Anita helped the others aboard the raft, and then they craned their necks upward to watch as the pilot lifted the helicopter out of the cone and flew away from the island.

Expedition Gaia had landed.

CHAPTER 5

All of Boat Team, including Skylar, the geologist, had thought that the water in the lake would calm down once the helicopter had left, that all of the churning had been due to rotor wash. They could see now, however, that this was anything but the case. All around them the lake—which was in fact ocean water that had been trapped in the center of the forming volcano cone—bubbled and sputtered, with gasses rising off of it giving the whole place an eerie, ethereal feel.

Skylar picked up the paddle, but seeing Anita reminded her that the professional explorer on Boat Team was an experienced boater, so she gave it to Anita. Skylar wondered if Anita might be irritated that Richard's comments about her boating experience were coming to pass, but these thoughts were interrupted by Anita, who asked, "Where to?"

All of them looked around, and Skylar produced a powerful flashlight to use as a search beam. She directed its illumination onto the jagged shoreline, sweeping the beam around in a clockwise circle.

While she did this, Joystna put her hand in the water. "Warm. About the same as the outside ocean water."

"That's because it is outside ocean water," Skylar said. "This subsea volcano formed underwater, and as it grew, it formed a caldera, a depression formed by the caving in of an empty chamber of magma. Then, seawater rushed in to take its place. It looks like an enclosed lake, or bowl of water, but it's most likely connected to the ocean through openings and chambers below the surface."

"Good to know it's warm in case we have to swim." Lara put a walkie talkie to her lips and spoke into it. "Boat Team to Slope, you copy?"

Static issued from the radio speaker but then Richard's English accent became decipherable. "We copy you, Lara. Still getting situated right where we got dropped off, but almost ready to move out. How's the boat?"

"Wet, but we're in it, safe and sound. Same situation here, basically, we're ready to move out."

Richard's laughter pealed out of the speaker, followed by the words, "Roger that, we'll check in later, then. Toodles!"

"So which way, then?" Anita asked again, paddle poised above the water.

"I don't see anywhere we can get out on so far." Skylar continued playing the torch beam around the volcano's interior. She studied the walls of the volcano leading up, narrowing as they reached toward the sky.

Joystna gazed up with what appeared to be trepidation. "All I can say is if we can't find a way out from in here somewhere, it's going to be one hell of a climb up. Either that, or we'll have to sit in this raft until the helicopter comes back to pick us up."

"Let's hope it doesn't come to that," Skylar agreed. "But it's a big island, and in my professional opinion, the chance that it's one hundred percent solid down here except for the lake is remote."

No sooner had she completed her sentence than Skylar steadied the search beam on an area of shoreline. "Look here." A narrow depression pockmarked the otherwise smooth surface of the curved shore.

"Looks like it could go back a ways. Let's check it out." Anita dug the oar into the water, paddling them toward the spot. As they progressed, a loose chunk of rock fell from somewhere high above on the inside volcano wall, making scraping sounds on the way down and finally splashing into the lake, a reminder that the brand new island was far from stable. Anita stopped paddling as they reached the mouth of an opening in the rocky wall of the lake chamber. Sheets of mist or vapor wafted from the surface of the lake, obscuring visibility into the opening.

"What do you think?" Skylar asked no one in particular.

Anita looked around the lake walls, seeing no other opportunities for exploration short of getting into full-on rock climbing. "I say we take the boat in a little ways and see where this goes, if anywhere."

The rest of the group voiced uneasy agreement, and Anita paddled the raft into the misty cave.

CHAPTER 6

Ethan Jones wiped his eyes again as he trotted ahead of the group so that he could turn around to snap a photo. He wanted an image to prove they were really here, boots on the ground, doing their job kind of thing. A public relations type shot. Document the expedition, that's what he was here for. But his eyes kept tearing up before he could compose his shot.

"Air up here is murder on the eyes."

Richard Eavesley led the Slope Team past Ethan along a rare horizontal section of the volcano's outer mountainside. "Sulfuric gasses coming from deep within the Earth. You should have thought to bring goggles. They're always a part of my kit." He made it a point to turn and look at Ethan with his plastic bug-eyes on.

"I see you're the only one wearing them. Thanks for letting the rest of us know," Ethan shot back. "Besides," he added quickly, deciding he'd come off a little harsh, "I couldn't really take good pictures with those on."

Richard didn't bother to turn around as he replied. "As I said, I didn't *know* I'd need them, they're merely one of those little things I make a point to carry in my kit. A you-never-know kind of item. They serve multiple purposes: safety goggles for fire-starting or working with tools, swimming goggles of course, because that's what they actually are, also protection against driving rain or snow…" He waved an arm at the vapor-shrouded landscape. "…or volcanic off-gassing. You just never, never know. Something over three decades of exploring has taught me."

Kai Nguyen, the translator, looked at Ethan and rolled his eyes as he marched by. Even he wore a bandana covering his mouth and nose, though. Ethan made a mental note to improvise something at the next rest stop, whenever that would be. What made Richard's remark sting a little, though, was that he did sort of kick himself for not having the foresight to be a little more prepared. He had trusted the U.N. bureaucrats too much. They had recommended only the most basic of gear types: climbing equipment, basic diving and snorkeling gear, camping stuff, communications, and so Ethan, deciding to travel light and that "less is more," did not augment that list. He had focused too much on his camera equipment to the exclusion of the expeditionary gear. Oh well. Next time.

George Meyer brought up the rear. Ethan thought he probably couldn't have heard the exchange, and he hoped not. But even if he was within earshot, the scientist was so engrossed in studying the surrounding geology that he may not have actually listened to any of it, anyway.

"I see the barest touch of lichens, I think they are, beginning to take root, already colonizing this new land. Do you mind?" He looked at Ethan's camera and then to a green patch on a rock.

"No worries, mate." Ethan knelt down and clicked off a few close-ups of the growth. He was just starting to stand up again when he heard Richard call out from up ahead. "Got something here!"

Ethan and the others ran to catch up with him but soon had to slow down in order to negotiate a winding path between two jagged lava rock walls. Through cracks in these, they could see orange lava still flowing deep inside the strata. The three trailing team members threaded their way through the passage and joined Richard, who was bending down next to an oval-shaped boulder the size of a small car.

Ethan was immediately taken with the sizable rock, and he began to photograph it. George, the geologist, was also intrigued.

"This is very different from the surrounding geology," the expert noted. Ethan began capturing video of the find, but Richard's voice stopped them cold in their tracks.

"Survivor!"

Ethan, George and Kai walked around to the other side of the boulder, where they saw Richard kneeling, eyes open wide as he stared at the base of the rock, where a human lay pinned beneath it.

The man was a Pacific Islander, with dark skin, a broad, flat nose and wild, bushy hair that was now streaked with ash. He was alive, but only just.

"Not sure how we're going to move him." Richard eyed the man's lower body. His legs protruded into a crevice, his feet eaten completely away by a lava pool there, his lower body having suffered horrific burns. The man muttered incoherently. He had clearly been trapped here for days, in this tortuous position, squeezed between jagged lava rocks and a huge boulder, splashes of running lava slowly burning him alive from the waist down. Forced to take nutrients the only way he could, he demonstrated how he had stayed alive, by licking the rough rock he could reach, to clear it of rain water and rocky nutrients. His tongue was swollen and bleeding from these efforts.

Ethan extended a canteen to the trapped survivor. "Here, water!"

Kai directed a question to him in Tongan, presuming him to be part of the Tongan landing party they had come to find. The man's eyes twitched in surprise upon hearing his native language, and he nodded before descending once again into nonsensical babbling.

Kai looked at the others. "He says he is part of the Tongan expedition."

Ethan reluctantly took photos of the trapped islander. It dismayed him to have to carry on with his work while someone suffered to such a degree, but this was absolutely something that needed to be documented, the state of a found survivor. Besides, Ethan thought, zooming in on the man's burned leg stumps, he wasn't sure what else he could do for him beyond providing water and food. He was wedged solidly beneath the boulder.

Richard and George began pushing against the big rock, while Kai explained to the man in Tongan that they were trying to free him. But the massive stone refused to budge. The two men stood back and reappraised the situation, out of breath, the skin on their hands torn from the brutal lava rock.

"Maybe if we fashion some kind of lever..." Richard suggested. No one said anything as the Tongan groaned, but George removed a rock hammer from his pack. "This is the longest tool at my disposal that might be used as a pry bar—anybody have anything better?" No one did, so he set about wedging it beneath the rock. Then he and Richard grabbed hold of the handle while Ethan and Kai pushed against the rock itself.

They lifted up on the handle to no avail. Still the rock would not move as the wooden handle creaked, threatening to break.

"Hold up." The geologist stood, catching his breath while eyeing the distressed Tongan. "I've got an idea." He bent down and retrieved his rock hammer. "Might as well try using this thing for what it's intended." He hefted the rock hammer, which featured a blunt striking surface and a tapered, lethal-looking pick at the opposite end. Then he approached the rock, eyeing it for the best place to start chipping away.

"Maybe I can crack it enough for you guys to be able to pull him out."

Everyone agreed, except apparently for the Tongan himself, who caterwauled loudly, waving his arms in the most frantic of motions his limited mobility would allow.

"Wait!" Kai raised an arm, and George backed off with the hammer. Kai leaned into the Tongan, who spoke his most coherent string of syllables thus far. Kai's face took on a confused expression, and he looked up at the others.

"He's still a little hard to understand, but from what I can tell he's worried about a…" He hesitated, as if unsure of how to phrase his next words.

"A what?" Richard prompted, slightly annoyed. The trapped man uttered some more words.

"…a 'devil beast.' I think he's saying that he doesn't want us to break the rock open."

Richard laughed and made eye contact with the Tongan, speaking in English. "Look, pal, you're in quite the situation, here. If we can't get this rock off of you—and soon—you're going to die, do you understand that?" He shifted his gaze to George. "Crack it apart if you can. It's his only hope."

George concurred and stepped up to the boulder once more with the rock hammer. He began striking the rock with the pick end of the tool. The Tongan screamed at him and shook his head.

"He's delirious from his ordeal. Keep going," Richard said calmly.

Kai told the man to relax, that they were doing their best to get him out, while George continued hammering. After a few minutes, a fragment of the boulder chipped away. George kept working the same spot, hoping he'd found a weak fissure to exploit. Meanwhile, Richard and Ethan pushed on the rock, still trying to budge it, hoping that each blow of George's hammer would be the one to loosen it enough to move.

The Tongan's protests, meanwhile, continued to fall on deaf ears.

A sizable hunk of rock fell away, and the boulder began to tip with the efforts of Richard and Ethan. "Almost there," Richard grunted. "Maybe one more piece, mate."

He and Ethan stepped away while George brought his hammer back for a big blow. Richard looked over at Ethan, saw the man resting with his hands on his knees, eyes closed for a moment while taking a much-needed breather. Seeing an opportunity, Richard stepped behind the nearest rock formation. He waited for two seconds to be sure no one would immediately call out his name, wondering where he went, or ask him to do something. Then he extracted a satellite-phone from his pocket, one whose existence was kept secret from the team. It had been given to him by Baxter, the CIA man.

Richard had accepted his offer that day in the British Explorers Club. Though he was not exactly wanting for money, his penchant for never-ending globetrotting excitement did not come cheap, and what the heck, he figured. There was that Italian villa he'd been eyeing for a vacation home to bring the missus to. This not-so-little bonus he'd worked out with Baxter would make that happen. He was going to the island anyway, so he might as well get more than the pittance the U.N. was paying him for doing the same thing, right? After a career of risking his hide in the far-flung corners of the planet, seeking out the highest reaches and dankest depths where most fear to tread (unlike most of his present company), he'd earned it.

Richard entered the passcode for the phone and then placed a call to the only number stored in its memory. As promised, Baxter himself answered, knowing who it was due to the dedicated number he'd assigned for this purpose.

"Hello, Richard. You have news?"

"Yes, but not much time to talk. Real quick: We found one of the Tongans. He's alive, but barely."

"Good! Then we know they made it there. Anyone else?"

"Not so far, only the one Tongan, but he's really bad off. I doubt he's going to make it, but we're doing our best to save him."

"Did he say what happened to the rest of them?"

"The translator's trying to get that out of him as we speak but he's pretty incoherent. The Tongan, I mean, not the translator."

"I can do without your lame attempts at humor, Richard. Can you—?"

At that moment, Ethan's voice called out from the boulder. "I think this next one's going to do it. Everybody get ready…"

Richard whispered into the phone. "Gotta go, mate. I'll be in touch."

"If this is the only survivor and he dies, make sure you drop those materials when you can, Richard."

"Copy that, out."

The explorer disconnected the call and pocketed the phone. He put his hands to his zipper like he was doing up his fly in a hurry as he came out from around the rocks, but it was a needless gesture since none of the team was looking his way.

Ethan swung the rock hammer in a two-handed grip, sideways through the air at full strength. It slammed into the side of the rock, above where the last chunk had been knocked loose, casting a spark—a tiny manmade speck of fire added to an island born of it.

That did it. The entire side of the boulder slid away, more than enough to allow it to be shifted. Ethan moved back into position at the boulder with his hands, where Richard joined him. Ethan was confident they'd be able to reposition the burdensome stone now that he'd chipped away at it some.

But before they placed their hands on the rock, it began to move on its own.

CHAPTER 7

Skylar played the light beam around the cave walls while Anita paddled the boat team deeper into the opening.

"This goes back quite a ways, and there's a fork in the road up ahead, too." Skylar illuminated a junction about a hundred feet away where two watery passageways led off to the right and left.

"Which way should we take?" Anita held her paddle poised over the water as the boat glided toward the fork.

"Let's try left." This from Lara who, as a communications expert, had no particular expertise in cavern navigation or volcanism. But to Skylar and Anita, it was as good a guess as any.

"Left it is." Anita dipped the paddle and angled the raft toward the left fork. The ceiling became lower as they entered the new tributary, and also more fractured. Veins of molten lava shimmered here and there behind the cave walls. Small offshoots led off to the right and left, a labyrinthine complex of magma chambers and lava tubes. Anita led them into one of these small side-chambers.

"Doesn't look like it leads anywhere," she said after paddling inside for some distance. "We should go back out to the main chamber." As she turned the raft around, Skylar played her light on the low ceiling, which she noted had a different composition than the jagged lava walls. While the other three women talked about which way they should turn the boat once they emerged from this chamber, Skylar took out a small rock hammer from her pack. As the raft passed beneath a particularly low-hanging section of ceiling that forced her to duck from her sitting position on one of the pontoons, she chipped away at a shiny inclusion. The others were laughing now about something, and none of them turned to see what she was hammering away at.

Just as the boat passed beneath the low section, the chunk of shiny rock fell into Skylar's left hand. Her headlamp reflected brilliantly from the specimen, which was breathtaking in its clarity, luminescence, lack of impurities, and most of all—its size. Skylar sucked in her breath as the realization of what she held in her hands hit her hard.

A diamond.

By far, the largest diamond specimen she'd ever encountered in both her professional—and personal—life. It was still raw, unprocessed ore and not a polished jewel, but still, the thing was damn near the size of a football! She looked up at the ceiling again, and even the upper walls of the cavern. Sparkles everywhere. Thick veins of the clear gemstone ran throughout the cave walls. A surge of adrenaline spiked through her body as she realized that this entire volcanic cave system was practically made of diamonds.

I was right! My research is confirmed.

But diamonds, of course, were not supposed to be her concern. She was here as a professional scientist, not a gem collector. But…wow! The diamond ore in this chamber alone would probably be enough to lower the worldwide asking price of diamonds were it allowed to flood the market all at once. Imagine, Skylar thought, rendering diamonds worth less than cubic zirconium, or even quartz! Not that she had the resources or ability on this little sortie to collect them all. That would require a full-fledged mining operation. No wonder the Pacific Island nations were fighting over this place so much, she thought. Perhaps they knew? She was aware that many times local people had knowledge of their environment that was not represented in the scientific corpus.

Then Anita was calling her name, asking her if they should go back and take the next right-hand fork along the main chamber. Skylar hurriedly dropped the huge hunk of diamond into her backpack. "Yes, yes. Let's check out that right fork."

"What are all those glittering stones?" Joystna asked on the way out.

They all looked to the geologist, who carefully dropped her pack to the bottom of the raft. "They're just mica deposits. They sure do look pretty, but they're not worth much at all."

CHAPTER 8

Ethan moved to the Tongan, believing the boulder was now rocking in place and about to fall back onto the imprisoned castaway. "It's moving. Pull him out of there before it falls back on him! Where were you, anyway, Richard?" The others bore confused looks as they stared at the wobbling rock.

"Sorry, had to take a leak. When you gotta go, you gotta go. So is this an earthquake? Is the island destabilizing?" Richard speculated. But nothing else around them was moving. And then, before anyone could answer, the giant rock transformed in the most unexpected, most brutal of ways.

An animal burst forth from the inside of the rocky covering. A living, breathing creature. A reptile, Ethan noted, hatching from an egg. Yet this wasn't any animal, nor was it simply a very large one. Ethan not only failed to take any pictures, such was the depth of his flabbergasted stupor, but he even let his best camera drop to the ground, the uncovered lens landing on a sharp piece of dried lava.

He didn't even notice the piece of terrible luck, something that would normally have him mentally calculating how many pictures he'd have to sell to replace the lens. In his mind's eye, he was taken back to his childhood, a childhood where video games and on-demand cable TV programming had yet to rule the day. Books had been Ethan's entertainment of choice. Even before he could truly read, he enjoyed looking at picture books, especially of animals. And of those, the ones about dinosaurs had been his favorite. Which was why now he recognized the creature standing in his midst as an ankylosaurus.

A dinosaur.

He didn't see how it could be possible. Were he in America or even Europe, he'd have guessed he was on the butt end of some kind of high-tech prank, or maybe an entertainment stunt for one of the nature channels he worked for. But way out here in the middle of nowhere? No one was going to bring some technological wizardry all the way out here. No way, no how. This was as real as it gets.

As if to emphasize that, the ankylosaurus began to move, first lifting its stout legs to clear the ruins of its protective cocoon, and then swinging its iconic tail weapon, that intimidating spiky ball Ethan remembered so well from his flashlight reading under the covers as a child. Also the rows of spiked armored plates along the back and sides. Unmistakable, yet at the same time unbelievable.

The primitive beast almost fell as it lurched forward in an attempt to remove one of its front legs from the rock. It lost its balance but did not topple. When its foot came down, however, it landed square on the head of the Tongan, crushing the man's skull. His brains slopped into a puddle of lava where they sizzled and burned, smelling like cooked meat for just a second before being consumed entirely, now a part of the island he had come to conquer on behalf of his nation.

"Look out, it's alive!" Ethan shouted while backpedaling without looking backwards—not a wise move in this environment, but preferable to being trampled by a prehistoric behemoth. A few steps back and he tripped over a lava rock spike, slashing his Achilles though not severing it, and landing him flat on his back, bashing both elbows on the razor sharp lava rock ground.

The nasty fall saved his life, for at that very moment, the ankylosaurus turned and trod across the spot where Ethan had been standing seconds earlier.

The photographer saw his camera with the cracked lens lying on the ground, and recovered enough to return his thoughts to photography, *Must. Get. Pictures! No one will ever believe this if I don't!* He reached into one of the many pockets of his vest and withdrew a small point-and-shoot digital job that he used as a backup or to frame quick compositions for reference. He'd never intended for it to shoot something so important, so utterly momentous, but things being what they were, it would have to do.

While Ethan lay there on the ground, activating his camera, the other team members scattered. Richard backed off slowly on the opposite side of the broken rock shelf, while George did the same not far from him, but calling out, "Fanbloodytastic, will you get a look at that! It's a bloody dinosaur!"

Richard paused behind a chest-high mound of rock, confident he was safe enough to rest here a moment as long as the ankylosaurus continued on its current path. He pointed to the animal's foot and ankle, where the Tongan's blood and cranial fluids dripped down the leg.

"It's a bloody dinosaur, all right. Literally, mate. Our Tongan friend is dead, skull crushed by that thing."

George blanched when he saw the lifeless, now headless form of the islander still slumped over the lava rock, transformed into nothing but an inanimate torso, his legs having been burned away and his head pulverized into innumerable skull fragments.

"We've got to—"

"Kai! Look out!" Ethan's yell cut George off. Ethan pointed to the ankylosaurus, which was in the midst of swinging its tail, the powerful biological mace at the end of it careening toward their translator.

Kai opted for a flat-out run over the uneven terrain, and whether the sudden rapid motion excited the beast, or if he simply was in the wrong place at the wrong time wasn't clear to Ethan. But when the heavy club slammed into Kai's upper back, impaling him with two of its spikes, none of that mattered anymore.

The translator, still stuck to the tail weapon, was flung through the air as the dinosaur thrashed about. The three Slope team members watched helplessly as their translator was flung into the rocky ground, bones breaking, blood spilling, before being dragged across the field of lava rock while the dinosaur thundered off. Then suddenly, it whirled back around, flipping its tail again like an irritated cat, the spiked man flying into the air along with it before being dashed to the ground once more, this time to his untimely death.

Having shed its club of the dead weight, the ankylosaurus gave a couple of flicks of its tail before running back toward the rock from which it had hatched. Richard and George flexed their legs, ready to run in whichever direction gave them the best chance of survival, while Ethan took video from his low profile position on open ground, afraid to move for fear of drawing the creature's attention.

The rampaging dinosaur settled into a straight course, a course that put it on a dead reckoning for George, who cowered between two jagged spires. Ethan didn't think the columns were anywhere near solid enough to withstand a hit from the marauding ankylosaurus, but he also didn't see what other options the geologist had. All around him was wide open space, until he got to Richard, a good thirty feet away. Didn't seem far, but when you were being run down by a galloping mega-lizard, every foot mattered.

George braced himself, putting an elbow in front of his face—a pathetic gesture really, when confronted with such a monstrous onslaught—when the ground suddenly opened up around the ankylosaurus and the huge animal sunk into a pit. It hung there for a few seconds, baying and caterwauling, an unnatural, otherworldly sound, until more rock slipped away and the beast dropped out of sight below.

Ethan rose, still taking video, and walked as close as he dared to the opened earth. He peered down into it, trying to see where the dinosaur had gone, if it would be able to get back up. Was it still a threat? But he could see they didn't need to worry about that.

"I can see the lake!"

"What?" Richard stuck his head out from around his lava rock cover.

"I'm looking down into the water in the middle of the volcano—the lake!" Ethan snapped off another photo down into the volcano.

"Where's that thing?" This from George, who tentatively emerged from his meager hiding spot.

"The dinosaur?"

"I guess that's what it is, yeah."

"Pretty sure it's an ankylosaurus. It fell into the lake. I saw it splash in. I don't think they can swim, so the Boat Team should be okay, as long as it didn't land on them."

At that, Richard and George began walking closer to Ethan's position where the dinosaur had plummeted through. They had nearly made it to the photographer again when the ground opened up once more, made less stable by what had already fallen through.

Richard's scream was the loudest, a feral shriek that would have done any haunted house justice on Halloween night. He slid down a suddenly created incline, bloodying his hands as he tried in vain to hold on, but gravity was too strong. He hit a protuberance at the bottom of the hanging section of volcano that served only to bounce him up into the air before he free-fell about fifty feet into the lake.

Popping and cracking noises erupted all around Ethan and George as the unstable slope continued to buckle. Ethan let his camera dangle by a neck lanyard, letting the video roll to capture what it might, but now concerned for his very life. He looked over at George to see the explorer pulling the Slope Team's satellite phone from his pocket. Time to call for help, people were dead. *Good thinking, George. We need help, we need to get out of here…*

But the ground opened up beneath George's feet again, and he was slammed onto his backside, jolting the phone from his hand. It bounced along the uneven terrain until it landed deep in a rocky fissure and wedged there. George scrambled to higher ground and stared down at the communications piece with terrified frustration. He looked back over to Ethan to see if he had witnessed what transpired. Ethan was watching, and the two made eye contact, the unspoken thought between them: No way to call for help without that thing. At least not until they reunited with Boat Team, who also had one. But they were somewhere down in the lake, and they needed help now.

George inched close to the crevice, reaching a hand out. "I think I can grab it."

"Forget it! We need to get clear of this area before—"

The volcano completed his sentence for him, the ground opening up completely in a wide circle around the two surviving men. George fell first, on his way to the lake while Ethan scrambled for a rocky pinnacle. He grabbed it, but then the entire base of the structure itself fell right through the sloped ground, and Ethan was free-falling to the lake.

CHAPTER 9

"This chamber looks very unstable. Keep us away from the walls." Skylar pointed to a horizontal orange streak moving behind cavern walls that were not yet fully solidified. Anita nodded, digging the paddle into the water on the right side of the boat, veering it away from the fiery wall. Around them, steam vented into the air from the water below, where magma still issued from deep within the Earth.

"I see a place it looks like we could get out on, over there." Lara put her radio away. She gave up trying to contact Slope Team since no signal could penetrate the cave walls. She pointed off to their right. Sure enough, a flat rocky shelf could barely be seen through the shroud of vapors. The others agreed to check it out, and Anita rowed them in that direction.

"There's water bubbling up over there!" Joystna indicated an area next to the rock shelf where the water roiled with frothy activity. "It's okay, just take us to the left of it," Skylar advised. "Don't go through the steam."

Anita guided them to the other side of the landing shelf from the active water. She paddled faster as she approached the ledge, and soon they heard the soft hiss of the raft's bottom sliding over the rock.

"Everybody out!" Anita said, jumping from the raft onto the rocky flat. "We don't want to puncture the boat bottom." The others hopped out of the boat, and they lifted it up onto dry ground before flipping on additional flashlights to have a look around.

The ceiling was low over half of the lava shelf, but high over the other half. The sounds of bubbling water and the occasional rock falling from high above echoed throughout the chamber.

The four of them spread out and walked toward the rear of the platform, looking for ways to get either further inside or higher up. They found neither. Skylar was in the midst of proposing a geological reason for this when she was interrupted by the sound of intense rushing water.

Anita pointed to what before had been a mere bubbly patch in the water, but now was a veritable geyser, shooting skyward with great force.

"Could this whole chamber flood?" Lara asked no one in particular. It was certainly an uncomfortable thought, to perish in this hellish cave system, crushed up against the chamber ceiling, clawing for the exit... Before anyone could give a response, a dark mass was buoyed up from the depths by the fountain of water.

"Stand back!" Joystna instinctively held her arm out to herd the others further from the edge of the platform, where a boulder was being lifted out of the water by the geyser.

The four explorers watched in disbelief as the large rock— perhaps the size of an overstuffed armchair—was tossed into the air. Then they covered their faces with their arms as the rock was smashed against the ceiling of the cave, casting off bits of rock shrapnel. The boulder landed on the rock shelf with a sonorous *crack*, wobbled for a second, and then settled.

They stood in place for a minute more, observing the geyser to see if it would throw up more projectiles from below, but the column of water gradually fizzled out, returning once again to the patch of bubbly water it had been when they arrived.

Curiosity got the better of Skylar, and she went to the big rock. She removed her rock hammer from her pack and struck the rock lightly until some of its surface layers chipped away. Lara moved closer behind her to shine a light on the work surface. As Skylar chipped away at the boulder, a thin vein of precious gemstone was uncovered. It sparkled hectically in the direct artificial light.

"What is that, more of that...what'd you say it was called?" Anita asked.

Skylar looked away from the rock for a second to frown in Lara's general direction, so she didn't see the boulder wobble slightly. "Mica. I'm not sure yet, need to get a better look..."

She resumed work again with the hammer, bringing the tool down near the mineral vein. Skylar cracked off a large sheet of the boulder and then paused with the hammer. She had opened up a sizable cavity so as to be able to reach in and try to excavate a chunk of what she was sure was diamond.

She had just passed her hand inside the cavity when the entire rock began to shake.

CHAPTER 10

Ethan wasn't sure which way was up. The water in the lake was dark. Adding to the confusion of being dumped underwater from about fifty feet up were the strange noises—the rumbling and popping of geological activity still at work as magma rushed out from the Earth. Spot fires burned around him underwater, adding to the surreal dream scene. Making matters worse, he still wore his pack, which threatened to pull him down into the abyss, however deep this body of enclosed water was. His plastic canteen bumped him in the face as it floated up, and that's when Ethan realized he was swimming the wrong way, down.

The photographer flipped himself around and kicked, straining against the weight of his backpack, but at the same time unwilling to ditch it except as a very last resort. He would be next to helpless on this island without his gear, and he couldn't be that far from the surface already, could he? A few seconds later, his face broke into humid air, and he gasped for precious breath, inhaling the sulfur-tinged atmosphere, air that had never tasted any sweeter to him than right now. But the triumph of figuring out how to keep breathing soon gave way to another predicament.

Where the heck was he? Ethan tread water while spinning in circles. Somewhere out in the middle of the lake. Looking up, he could see the main opening of the volcano, as well as a smaller aperture to one side of it—the new hole where he had fallen through with the collapsing slope rock. He heard splashing to his right. Hoping it wasn't the ankylosaurus swimming for him— surely it sank by now?—he looked over to see a person splashing toward him.

"Ethan? George?" a male voice called out.

"Ethan here, Richard." Ethan couldn't yet see the man as anything more than a blurry form, but he recognized the English accent.

"Any sign of George?" Richard swam over to Ethan, and the two of them looked around until they heard another voice, a little farther away from Ethan than Richard had been.

"Over here!" They spun in the direction of the words. Just visible through the mist were a pair of waving arms.

"George?" Ethan called.

"Yes, it's me." George started swimming and soon disappeared into the fog.

"Wrong way, George. Turn around," Ethan said.

The geologist, disoriented in the misty vapor, spun around until he was looking in the right direction. Richard activated a waterproof flashlight, and then George homed in on that with ungainly, splashy kicks. While they waited for him to reach them, Ethan and Richard looked around at their surroundings. They were far from the shore of the lake on all sides, near the middle. George reached them, and they asked one another if they were okay. All had cuts and bruises but nothing major; thankfully, all three were able to swim.

Richard, still wearing his pack, removed it and took from it a two-way radio. "Glad we sprung for the waterproof model now, right, mates?" Ethan nodded, but George looked around briefly. "I lost my pack. I wasn't wearing it when the ground fell through."

"Don't worry about that right now. You're still alive. I'm sure Kai would like to be in your position, precarious as it may be at the moment." Richard pulled the radio from a compartment of his pack. "Ah, here we are. Let's see if we can raise our Boat Team, perhaps we can arrange to be picked up. They must be putting about in here somewhere, right?"

Ethan spun about in a slow circle. "I don't see or hear them..." Then he cupped his hands together and yelled through the vapors. "Skylar? Anita? Lara? Joystna?"

They waited a moment for the echoes to die down, but when no reply was forthcoming, Richard held up the radio. "Let's give this a try, shall we?" He depressed the Talk button and spoke into the radio's microphone. "Slope Team to Boat, Slope Team to Boat, do you read, over?"

A few seconds passed during which nothing, not even static, was heard. "You on channel 22?" Ethan asked.

Richard nodded. "Affirmative, I'm on 22. That's what they should be on." He tried the radio again, telling boat team they had fallen into the lake, lest they think the reason for the call was routine and were ignoring it. But still no response came.

"Why can't we reach them? Shouldn't they be in the lake? That's where we dropped them, right?" George's voice sounded as though he was on the verge of panic.

Richard leveled a stare at him. "Lots of reasons why it might not work. Signal could be bouncing all around down here, maybe they entered a cave along the shore, who knows?"

Richard shook his head as he clipped the radio off to a shoulder strap on his pack. "I'll leave it on, but I think we're going to have to take matters into our own hands at this point."

All three of them once again surveyed the lake. "You mean swim for shore, right?" George asked.

Richard laughed. "Uh, yeah, unless you have some magical way out of here, or you know how to fly or something."

"Hey, no need to be an ass about it, I was just—"

"Take it easy, mates." Ethan tried to sound upbeat. "We're all in this together, and we're all going to get out of this together. So let's figure out which way the shore is closest, then we'll start our little power swim, okay?"

Richard shone his light beam straight toward the shore in the direction he faced. "You gentlemen still have your lights?"

Ethan felt around the outside of his pack until he found his. He unclipped it and then flicked it on, leveling the beam in the opposite direction from Richard.

"I don't have a light. It was in my pack." George sounded downbeat.

"I'm guessing about a quarter-mile in this direction." Richard waved his light against the lava rock shore. "But it's hard to say for sure." Ethan turned around to look, comparing the distance to shore in the opposite direction, where the vapors were thicker. "I think your way is closest."

"Let's get on with it, then, before more crap falls on us from above, or more magma pushes up from below." Richard clipped his light back on to his pack but left it on as a beacon for the others, so that they could find one another if separated. Ethan did the same with his light, and the three of them swam toward shore.

Ethan felt the weight of his wet pack on his shoulders as he kicked along, noting that Richard must feel the same. Only George lacked a pack, and for that reason, he was the fastest among them. It was strange to need the lights to see the shoreline, yet the center of the lake was bathed in daylight. Sunlight at this time of day penetrated straight down, leaving a cone of light in the middle of the lake and the surrounding shore in darkness. As they passed through the cone of sunshine, Ethan saw George stop swimming up ahead. At first, he thought it might be because he was afraid of getting too far ahead of Ethan and Richard, for to lose them would mean he was on his own with no equipment in the dark volcano.

But then George spoke. "Something touched me."

"Keep swimming, George, don't freak yourself out." Richard heeded his own advice, transporting his heavy pack via his lumbering crawl stroke.

"Probably just some floating debris, maybe a cooled magma pillow drifting around the lake," Ethan offered.

"I'm a geologist, Ethan, so while I appreciate you trying to make me feel better, I —"

Suddenly, George was pulled underwater in a swift and violent motion. The water roiled and then an object of some kind was seen breaking the water's surface.

"What is that?" Richard gasped, halting his forward progress to tread water.

Ethan, being an experienced nature photographer, had an idea, but not one that made him feel any better. "Some type of creature, mate. I don't know what kind, but that looked like a flipper or fin."

"Great, we have a shark in here?"

Before Ethan could answer, an enormous dark mass arced up out of the water—an animal in a breaching dive. To Ethan, it looked sort of like a whale, except it had four flippers instead of two, and it had a *neck*, a long, thin neck…at the end of which was a head with sharp teeth that had George Meyer, the geologist, clenched between the jaws. The man screamed wordlessly as he was taken into the air for the final time. Then the animal dove underwater with its prey and disappeared.

Richard shifted his light from the position where the creature had dived to the shoreline, sweeping it across the rockscape, seeking the closest point of escape.

"Let's go!" Forgoing stealth in favor of top speed, Richard launched into a flurry of windmilling arms and kicking legs, propelling himself toward the rocks. Ethan kept his light trained on the spot where he last saw the creature, his mind's eye picturing it launching itself out of the crater lake...and he was a kid again, looking at those dinosaur books... *I know this one...plesiosaur*! But attaching a name to the beast didn't provide additional comfort. In fact, the opposite proved to be true, since he knew that plesiosaurs were formidable marine predators.

Ethan stopped looking for George and his plesiosaur and struck out after Richard and the shoreline. It seemed impossibly far away when being chased by a primordial monster, but he told himself that if the dinosaur wanted to take him, it was going to take him regardless of his actions in the water. The only thing he could do was to get out as fast as possible so that he wasn't around when the creature finished swallowing George. What if it decided that wasn't half bad and went looking for more?

Ethan stopped swimming when Richard aimed his light back at him, waving the beam back and forth. "I see a ledge I think we can get up on over there." He jiggled the light beam off to their left. Ethan moved off in that direction, expecting to feel a powerful set of jaws tugging at his legs at any moment. But he reached Richard without that happening, and the professional explorer surprised him by handing him his torch.

"Hold this, will you, and aim it up there so I can get out. Then I'll pull you up."

Ethan hesitated for a split second. *Wonder what he'd say if I said I would go first?* But he didn't want to prolong his stay in the lake a microsecond more than was necessary, plus the ledge was a couple of feet of razor sharp lava rock above their heads and wouldn't be all that easy to climb out on. Ethan wouldn't mind being pulled out, at the cost of being second. He took the light.

Richard eyed him hard for a moment, then nodded and turned around.

"Right here," he said, pointing. "Shine it right here."

Ethan complied, and the Brit began to climb. He made it about three feet up and was stretching an arm out onto level ground when he suddenly fell back, splashing into the water next to Ethan. He cried out in pain, and Ethan's first thought was that somehow the plesiosaur had struck Richard instead of him, even though Richard had been mostly out of the water until one second ago. But then Richard let loose a string of oaths and shrugged out of his pack.

"That was stupid, I should have known to take my pack off first. Also, let me don my climbing gloves. This stuff is like trying to climb a wall of razor blades."

Ethan shined the light as the explorer unzipped a side pouch on his bag and took from it a pair of gloves. He put them on and shoved the pack over to Ethan. "Just hold it there until I get up, and then I'll pull it up, okay?"

Ethan nodded. He had already removed his own pack and so now floated with two of them while shining the light. But the extra work paid off, as this time Richard scaled the ledge without incident, hauling himself out and taking a brief look around. Then he turned back to Ethan, extending a hand. He pulled up first his backpack, then Ethan's. The photographer had to admit that as pompous as the explorer was, he was quick and efficient in his movements once he selected the proper gear. He was not leaving Ethan to dangle in the water a second longer than necessary.

"You're going to have to brace your feet against the side— there's a little cutout—there, yes. Now get a good grip..." He held out a hand and Ethan held on.

"Up you go..." Richard pulled, and Ethan was able to take a couple of vertical steps up until he could step up onto the horizontal ledge. He eyed the explorer in the misty, dim light.

"Thanks."

Richard nodded, then aimed his light behind them. "Now then, where are we?"

CHAPTER 11

Ethan finished changing into dry clothes and then shouldered his pack. Richard had done the same, and now he took the two-way radio to the edge of the shelf. He spoke into it, trying to raise the Boat Team, but no response came. Ethan shook his head as he played his beam out across the lake.

"I don't see any sign of the boat, either. I wonder if that plesiosaur got them, too?"

"Even if it got them, I doubt it would eat the entire raft, too. And even shredded, those rafts float, there would be some sign of things floating around somewhere."

Ethan shrugged. "So what do you think happened to them?"

"They must have found a passage into a cave. That would also explain why we can't make radio contact. And remember, we saw that life vest floating down here before we landed. It probably came from the Tongan party, and they came by boat, so it's possible that there is a passage to the outside from the lake."

"I guess we'll have a look around, then. If we can't find the rest of the team, then maybe we can find a way topside, which we're going to have to do anyway at some point."

Richard agreed, and the two men walked back along the narrow ledge—perhaps twenty feet or so—to where it met the volcano's internal wall, which was solid with no opening of any kind. They began making their way around the perimeter of the roughly circular lake by walking along the ledge, counter-clockwise. Ethan walked lakeside, sweeping his beam across the water in search of any sign of the Boat Team, while Richard patrolled the wall, looking for dry passages that led off the shelf.

They picked along in this way until Richard called out that he had found something. "Over here. Looks like a cave."

Ethan joined him at the rear of the shelf, and the two men shone their lights inside a cleft in the rock that was perhaps head high and ten feet wide.

"Looks like it might jog to the right, back there." Richard waved the light back and forth to illuminate the far end of the cave.

"Let's check it out." Ethan stepped inside, had a brief look around in the main chamber, and then walked to the rear of the cave. To his right was a cul-de-sac, dead-ending about thirty feet further inside. Richard added his beam to the back wall, scanning it left to right until he froze it in place.

"See that?" A pile of something—sticks maybe, or rocks—lay in a heap at the rear of the cul-de-sac.

Ethan and Richard moved to the rear of the chamber. Ethan froze in mid-step when he got close enough to identify what he was looking at on the cave floor. "Those are bones."

Richard nodded, walking right up to the pile and kneeling in front of it so as to get a better look. "Human bones, at that."

Ethan took his point-and-shoot camera from his vest only to find it was soaking wet and now useless. He opened his pack and then dumped the non-working camera inside in case what pictures he had already taken could be retrieved later.

"Should have just used this one all along," he thought, taking out a waterproof camera meant for scuba diving. He didn't know if diving would be necessary on this trip, but in his experience, it paid to be prepared. To that end, he'd brought along a compact scuba rig. It took up precious space and weight in his pack, but he was glad he had it, if nothing else for the underwater camera that went with it. He'd already lost two cameras on this trip. He needed something rugged that would hold up to the elements here. Then he chided himself for being so petty. *At you haven't lost your life, like Kai and George.* He pictured Kai being tail-slammed by the ankylosaurus and George being consumed in the jaws of the plesiosaur.

Ethan clicked off a few pictures of the bones, the camera's flash dazzlingly bright in the cave lit only by two flashlights. He lowered his camera and studied the bones with his naked eyes. "Do you think…?"

"They're pretty recent. No meat, though, and many are cracked in half or totally pulverized. Like something massive just went to town on them."

"Right, like a dinosaur or dinosaurs. But do you think these are from more of the Tongans in the landing party?"

Richard grabbed a bone and used it as a stick to topple part of the pile, exposing more facets of the remaining bones. "It would have to be confirmed by an anthropologist, I would think. I can say with certainty that these are human bones. Look at the skull there. But I am definitely not qualified to tell one race apart from another."

"The skull is weirdly clean, though, for recent bones, isn't it? No skin or flesh of any kind." Ethan snapped some more shots of the newly uncovered bones and skulls.

Richard looked around the cave, at the walls, which were solid lava rock, with a couple of large rocks in one corner. He placed a hand on the nearest wall. "Still warm. We're standing in a magma chamber formed by hot lava. It's quite possible that the bones were submerged in lava for a time, which would remove all traces of flesh."

Ethan was about to reply when one of the rocks against the wall began to crack apart on its own. At first, he thought the cave was collapsing, but as he watched, he understood that only the one rock was being affected. It happened so fast that neither man had time to run. One second they were looking at the rock, and the next, it had burst open, releasing a head-high reptile.

The lizard was thin and spry, very agile even right out of its cocoon.

Richard froze stock still. Ethan wasn't sure if he was trying out some motion-vision trick on the beast's eyes or if he just didn't know what to do, but either way, Ethan sensed that the outcome wouldn't be good. A little voice in Ethan's head couldn't resist telling him what he was looking at: *Velociraptor.*

Another dinosaur. Fast. Meat-eater. Thought to hunt in packs…before he could recall more facts, the reborn lizard began tentatively snapping its jaws, as if awakening after a very long time and reacquainting itself with its basic functions.

CHAPTER 12

Skylar withdrew her hand from the big jewel-laced rock just as it split in half. She stepped back—in surprise, not fear. Did she not know her own strength with the rock hammer? As a professional geologist, using that tool was second nature to her. She was certain she hadn't struck the specimen too hard or at a structural weak point. So then what was happening? Did the mineral possess some unique lattice structure that caused it to fracture easily?

Joystna, Lara, and Anita were crowded around the rock behind her to see what was inside the strange boulder that had been spit from the lake by a geyser. The two halves fell to the cave floor, leaving a dust-covered form in between them. At first, Skylar mistook it for part of the rock.

But then it started to move.

Anita screamed. Joystna backed up, putting distance between herself and the strange spectacle playing out before them. Lara simply turned around and fled as fast as she could toward the rear wall of the cave.

Leaving Skylar face to face with an adult pterodactyl.

The bird-like lizard stamped its feet and squawked once, a hideous screeching noise. The sound awoke Skylar to the fact that this was absolutely not part of a rock. The pterodactyl pecked at Skylar, its hard beak jabbing at the geologist's forearm, drawing blood. She yelled incoherently, a wordless reaction to the primeval assault.

Then the ptero lunged at Skylar again, putting its whole body into it this time, enveloping her with its leathery wings while batting at her head with its two-foot-long beak. Still holding the rock hammer, Skylar brought it up as hard as she could, but one of the creature's wings restricted her movement. Still, the metal head struck the animal in the side of its neck, eliciting a sharp squawk accompanied by a jumping motion that took the ptero off of her.

It landed a few feet away on flat ground, in the midst of the four dumbstruck women. The ptero turned in little jumping circles, hopping slightly while turning its body in mid-air so as to give itself a 360-degree view of its new surroundings. Millions of years of evolution, awakening. Even after a slumber of eons, the animal's genes knew what to do. It began to strike out in exploratory pseudo-flights, hopping high into the air while flapping its wings before landing back on the ground and pushing off again.

On one of these hops, it flew out over Lara, who had reached the end of the lava shelf with nowhere to go other than the lake. The ptero body slammed her, hitting her sideways with its wing. She teetered and then splashed into the lake while the flying reptile wheeled back for another pass across the ledge. Fortunately for Lara, the edge of the shelf was not high up from the lake at this point, and so she was able to scramble up and out of the water, though not without an assortment of deep cuts and severe scrapes. She hunkered down on the edge of the shelf while the winged dinosaur continued to rampage on the ledge.

The ptero bumped against the cave wall and then corrected with a howl, turning out toward the lake while flying about six feet above the ledge. Anita ducked as the predator passed over her head, and Skylar threw a hunk of its cocoon rock at it, hitting it in the side.

The ptero turned to the right after being struck, passing back over the ledge, where Joystna stood, hopping back and forth from leg to leg as if unable to make up her mind in which direction to go. The ptero suffered no such indecision, however, and barreled towards her, mouth agape.

From Skylar's vantage point at the cracked rock the beast had hatched from, it looked as though a model airplane or something powered was on a collision course with the doctor. Skylar hefted another chunk of rock to use as a defensive missile, but she was too late. The pterodactyl closed its beak around Joystna's neck and continued to fly along the back wall of the ledge, dragging the doctor with it.

Choking and gasping sounds issued from Joystna's throat while the creature carried her along, her feet dragging across the rough lava rock, ankles tearing apart on the spiky surface. Lara ducked as the creature passed over her. She grabbed Joystna's legs and the three of them—communications specialist, doctor, and pterodactyl—were dragged to the ground at speed. But Lara couldn't hold on when her thigh struck a jagged lava protrusion, and the ptero peddled its legs over the ground while still dragging its prey.

Skylar hurled another rock at the winged marauder. It bounced off the monster's thick hide, knocking into Joystna on its way to the ground. Skylar picked up another projectile and put her arm back to throw, but then halted. Something was wrong. Joystna. She was still now, unmoving, legs no longer pedaling to seek purchase, and her head... Skylar choked back rising bile as she saw the sick angle at which the physician's neck now lay in the beak of the beast.

Then the pterodactyl took to the air again, Joystna still in its terrible grip, this time not stopping when it got to the edge of the lava shelf, but continuing to fly out over the lake. It banked into a turn while continuing to rise, circling as it flew ever higher, toward the distant circle of light at the roof of the volcano. When it reached a lofty height above the lake, out of sight from the ledge, the ptero emitted a shriek that echoed across the water.

Then the three remaining members of Boat Team saw Joystna's body plummet down from out of sight above, falling until she landed on the lava shelf on the opposite side of the lake, the crack of the medical doctor's bones echoing in the hollow volcano.

CHAPTER 13

"What the hell is that thing?" Richard rasped. Before him, on the floor of the cave, stood a bipedal lizard with a mouthful of razor sharp teeth and unblinking black eyes devoid of personality.

"I think it's a...uh...a velociraptor." Ethan raised his camera and snapped off a shot of the freak of nature, careful to keep his movements slow and unthreatening, though he'd have to take his chances with the flash. Hopefully, that would have an intimidating effect, if anything.

"A vel—isn't that a dinosaur?" The explorer's voice was shrill.

"Yeah, Richard. Isn't that what it looks like? "

For once, Ethan thought, the Brit had no snarky retort. The photographer's silent gloating was cut short, however, when the raptor thrust its head out at Richard. It snapped its jaws where the geologist's face had been one second earlier. Then, without waiting to further assess the capabilities of its prey, the dinosaur jumped to one side, lashing out with a leg and slamming its clawed foot squarely into Ethan's chest.

The impact sent him reeling backwards into the cave wall. His shirt tore as the raptor pulled its foot back and the claws ripped through the fabric. The reptile pecked at Ethan's face, and he reeled back, just out of reach. Then, its attention span seemingly at its limit for any single task, the velociraptor spun and leaped across the breadth of the cave in a single bound, landing on Richard again.

"Help me, Ethan!" Richard bellowed as the beast sunk its teeth into his exposed side. Richard tried reaching down to his pack, which he'd taken off and set on the ground when they'd reached the cave, where he had a machete in a sheath tucked into some webbing on the outside. But the animal knocked him to the ground before he could reach it and began ravaging the man, biting into him and tossing its head back and forth with blinding speed.

Ethan ran to the dinosaur with his head lowered. He rammed the beast in the side like a football linebacker, feeling a spray of Richard's blood land on his face as the velociraptor whirled around in surprise, reacting to this new threat.

Richard wasted no time in taking advantage of this saving grace, the distraction Ethan had provided. He rolled away from the dinosaur and swiped his machete from his pack. While the raptor faced off with Ethan, Richard rose to his feet and raised the long blade high over his head in a two-handed Samurai stance. He brought the machete down while the dinosaur was leaning over Ethan, who was kicking it in the face with his steel-toed hiking boots.

The blade sunk into the dinosaur's back for half its length. The beast hissed and spun around so fast that its tail slammed into Richard's upper body and sent him flying—feet clear off the ground—until he hit the cave wall and slumped to its floor. Behind the raptor, Ethan had scooped up a sizable chunk of rock, preparing to launch it at their attacker.

But the raptor had had enough. It loped out of the cavern, bleating like a wounded animal, the machete still protruding from its back.

Ethan moved to Richard, whose midsection was dark red with copious amounts of thick blood. The explorer held his hands together over his stomach. Ethan knelt down next to him.

"Let me take a look, mate." He was terrified he'd see guts spilling out of the man once he took his hands away, but Ethan was relieved to see it wasn't quite that serious. The wound was definitely bad, though, a deep gut opening and bleeding heavily. Not only that, but it wasn't the only one. Another gouge almost as large marred his upper thigh, and numerous smaller cuts peppered his body as though he'd been beaten with rakes.

Ethan ran to his pack and removed a first-aid kit. He cleaned and sterilized the wounds as best he could and then bandaged them, but the gauze soaked through with blood almost immediately. He didn't think a tourniquet could be applied to a mid-section wound, but wasn't sure. The only thing he was sure of was that they needed the doctor, and fast. He handed Richard a couple of painkillers and a bottle of water. Richard washed back the pills and leaned his head against the rock wall.

"Christ almighty, we have to get out of here. Between the Tongan we found half-alive, and those guys over there," he said, nodding to the bones, "we know what happened here."

Richard tried to get to his feet. Ethan assisted him, and he had to pause once, but eventually he was able to take steps on his own. Ethan carried the explorer's pack for him, while wearing his own on his back.

"Don't worry, mate. As soon as we reunite with Boat Team, the doc will patch you right up."

CHAPTER 14

Skylar watched Lara fiddle with her walkie-talkie. "Still nothing?"

The comm tech shook her head, turning a knob on the radio. "I thought maybe if I adjust the squelch so that…" Static emanated from the tinny speaker. "There! Hold on…"

Lara pressed the Talk button. "Boat Team to Slope, do you read?" She held her fingers over the controls, occasionally fine-tuning the settings. For a while, the static dropped out, and silence ruled the channel during which Anita's quiet sobs seemed like the loudest thing on the island. Then the static returned, this time with a scratchy human voice.

Lara tapped a control and spoke into the radio. "Boat Team, you out there?"

"…read you…hurt."

A frustrating minute went by during which the two radio operators struggled to improve their signal. Finally, Slope Team was clear enough to hear. "Lara here. Who am I talking to? Is that Ethan?"

"Yes, it's me. Listen, glad we made contact, but I need to cut right to the chase. We have had two deaths, I repeat, *deaths* caused by strange animals, over."

Skylar exchanged a glance with Lara. "Say again, Ethan. Did you say 'deaths caused by animals'?"

"Affirmative."

"We've had that problem, too. One dead. Listen: we're near the edge of a cave system right now, on the lake shore but under a large overhang, near the water level. Where are you?"

A burst of static garbled his transmission, then he was audible again. Lara asked him to repeat his last message.

"We're also somewhere down along the lake, but in a cave system. We're almost out of it. Our progress is slow because

Richard has been seriously injured, but we'll make it out to the lake, over."

Skylar raised her eyebrows. "They're down here? Ask them how they got down here."

Lara nodded. "Thought you guys would still be topside on the outer slope. Looks like you found a good way down. We're looking for a way up ourselves, so maybe we can follow you guys back outside?"

Ethan's reply was immediate. "Sorry to tell you, but we're looking for a way up out of here, too."

Lara looked confused as she spoke into the walkie. "But I thought you said—"

"Let's just say we didn't mean to drop in on you like this, but it happened. Fill you in on the details when we meet up."

"Okay, Ethan—listen up: move out to the edge of the lake so that we can see each other—flash a light—and we'll have a stronger radio signal."

"Copy that. On our way now. Over and out."

Lara clipped the radio back onto her belt and looked at Skylar, who in turn eyed Anita, now wiping tears from her face.

"You ready to go, Anita?" The sailor nodded.

Lara pointed toward the end of the ledge. "We should head out there and get out from under this overhang. Hopefully, they're already on this side of the lake, but we'll see."

Wearily, Anita got to her feet and shouldered her pack. The three women started to walk toward the end of the ledge, but Lara stopped when they came to Joystna's backpack.

"We should take her pack."

"I don't want to carry it." Skylar kept walking.

Lara raised her voice. "We don't have a doctor anymore, but we could at least redistribute her medical supplies so that we have those."

"She's right." Anita shrugged off her pack and knelt down next to the dead physician's bag. She opened it and began taking out the medical supplies and equipment. She and Lara began stuffing their own packs with the medical gear while Skylar stood and watched from a distance.

"Come on, Skylar. There's lots of stuff here. We should take her other gear like flashlights and tools, too, if we can. Come over and put some of this stuff in your pack, please. We might need it later."

Skylar frowned in Lara's direction. "All right. One minute, let me organize some room in my pack." The geologist knelt behind the fragments of the rock the pterodactyl had hatched from. Then she remembered. She turned her head to look at the inside of the rock that somehow acted as an egg for the dinosaur. Maybe like a *cyst*, Skylar mused. But she could take that up with the biologists later. Right now what concerned her was not leaving behind all those glittering hunks of high-grade diamond ore.

She looked back at her fellow expedition members and saw the growing pile of medical kit gear Lara and Anita were stacking off to one side—Skylar's share of the increased burden she would have to take on if they had any hope of providing their own medical care whatsoever—that she was supposed to put in her pack. She had to be able to take all that stuff or they would get suspicious, she thought, scooping diamonds into the deep bottom part of her backpack, on top of the football-sized specimen she already had. *Have to do something better with these the next time I can, put them inside something, but this will have to do for now...*

She saw a small collapsible shovel she hadn't used yet and removed it from the pack, laying it beneath some crumbled rock pieces. *Probably won't need this thing, anyway.* She did the same with a coil of climbing rope. *This is just my extra rope, anyway, I also have a main set, so out with this, too...* She repeated this process a couple of more times with different types of expeditionary gear, then sat back on her haunches, grinning while she looked into her bag. *Plenty of room now.*

Skylar grabbed two more fistfuls of raw diamonds and dropped them into the bag before standing, picking up her pack and walking over to Lara and Anita at the medical pack. She began transferring the pile of medical supplies into her own backpack.

Anita looked over at Skylar while they stowed the new supplies into their packs. "I know you're a geologist and not a biologist, but still, you're a scientist. How do you think it's possible that that...pterodactyl, right? That it got here?"

Skylar shrugged. "My best guess is that the 'rocks' are not really true rocks at all, but actually some kind of pods, or cysts, that protected the animals inside over the millennia. Until today, when they experienced sufficient trauma through the volcanic processes that created this island to break apart and hatch."

"But baby animals hatch, like birds that start out as chicks. That pterodactyl was fully grown, though."

"How do you know?"

Anita looked up from her pack, suddenly embarrassed. More than embarrassed...there was another emotion there, too—fear. "Well, I've seen pictures—"

"You've seen pictures that are artists' guesses as to how they looked. We're probably the first humans ever to lay eyes on a living pterodactyl. What if this..." She pointed over to the broken cyst, mentally cautioning herself not to draw too much attention to her private diamond mine. "...*is* the size at which they hatch, and they only grow bigger from here on out?"

Anita exhaled heavily through her nose, but it was Lara who put words to the situation. "Bones, right? Fossils? Don't those tell us the size?"

Skylar nodded as she dropped a roll of gauze into her bag. "They definitely help, but the fossil record is by no means complete. What if—?"

But Lara waved a hand, cutting her off as if suddenly frustrated. "Let's not think about all that just yet, okay?" She held up the satellite phone before dropping it back inside her pack. "We only need to be here long enough to reach the outer slope, where we'll have a clear signal for the sat-phone, and then we'll call the U.N. for an early extraction."

Skylar grimaced under the weight of her pack, laden with stones.

"You okay, Skylar?" Anita glanced at the geologist's legs with concern.

"Oh yeah, I'm fine. Just a little leg cramp, that's all. Ready to move out."

Anita's gaze lingered a few seconds more, this time on Skylar's pack itself, probably to see if she had it adjusted right, Skylar thought. *Gotta get used to this heavy load fast or they'll want to redistribute my gear…*

Lara's voice broke Skylar's train of thought. "Okay, we've got everything. Let's see if we can get out from under this ledge and make contact with the rest of our team."

Lara walked off toward the end of the ledge while Skylar wondered how long she should let her think she was in charge.

CHAPTER 15

Ethan was grateful to see the lake water ahead of him. It meant they had finally emerged from the maze-like cave system they'd been exploring. He and Richard, who had slowed the pair down considerably but was able to move himself along with Ethan carrying his pack, leaned against a shallow ledge while they looked out on the lake. As before, a circular cone of sunlight fell upon the middle of the water, with the edges in near darkness.

Ethan had concerns about Richard's physical outlook but knew they only had to get topside. Then they could use a sat-phone to request a helicopter pickup. That's how he hoped things would unfold, anyway, but he had traveled to enough remote parts of the planet photographing nature to know that what he hoped for and what would actually come to pass were oftentimes not one and the same.

Still, they had a working plan, and he would stick to it. He flipped on both his headlamp and a handheld flashlight, the beam of which he began sweeping around the lake shore, illuminating the dark reaches where sunlight did not fall. Richard wordlessly did the same. Their four lights swept the lake's surface and shoreline as they searched for signs of Boat Team.

Ethan had just raised the radio to his lips when Richard pointed. "There!"

Ethan turned in time to see a bluish-tinted xenon bulb flashing on the opposite lake shore. He clicked the button on his flashlight three times until it entered strobe mode, and pointed it toward Boat Team's light. In return, he received a flashing pattern from across the lake.

He held the Talk button on his radio and spoke into it. "Slope team to Boat, you copy?"

"Yes!" The reply was shouted across the lake, not transmitted through the radio.

"Good to hear your voice, Lara." And Ethan meant it. He would never admit it to anyone, least of all Richard, but the isolation was getting to him. He found it mentally uplifting to hear another human voice besides Richard's without the aid of a radio. Then the voice issued through the speaker.

"Okay, so we see each other. What's the best way to meet up? Seems like a long way to try to walk all the way around, if that's even possible. Feel like swimming?" The last question was meant to be a joke, but Richard literally groaned at the thought. The matter of what lived in the lake's dark waters didn't sit well with Ethan, either, not after what had happened to George. Ethan forced an image of the plesiosaur out of his mind while he replied.

"What about the raft, do you still have it?"

"We beached it up on the shore a little ways from here, to our left as we're facing you. But it's not all that far. We could get it and then row across to your location. Does that sound like a plan?"

Ethan looked over at Richard, who nodded vigorously.

"Sounds like a plan, Lara. We'll be right here, and I'll be standing by on this channel, over."

Ethan thought he could hear what sounded like arguing—angry female voices—across the lake. But the lights began moving off toward the raft, so he didn't ask about it. Truth be told, he and Richard needed them more than he and Richard were needed, no doubt about that. If push came to shove, Boat Team had a sat-phone, they had climbing gear. They could get out of here without the decimated Slope Team if they had to. Richard, meanwhile, could barely move without Ethan's help.

"Sounds like they're arguing about something." Richard set his flashlight on a rock so that it pointed toward the boat team without him having to hold it, a fixed beacon.

"Can you make out what they're saying? I can't."

"I can't either. Not that I give a damn as long as they get over here. I'm going to take a nap while we wait, Ethan." Richard adjusted his pack so that he could lean against it.

"Suit yourself. I'll be right over here, having a little snack." Ethan climbed up onto a flat plateau about six feet above the ledge he and Richard occupied. He thought it might give him a better vantage point from which to monitor Boat team's progress across the lake.

A few minutes later, Ethan heard the sound of Richard snoring and looked over to see the famed explorer catching some Zs with his head propped against his pack, standing on one leg with the other laid out flat on a ledge. Ethan felt a little guilty that he couldn't find a way to get him up here, where there was ample room to really stretch out and relax, but damned if he was going to haul his ass up here.

He was considering tossing a pebble on the man to see if it might disrupt his snoring without waking him up, when he became aware of a different sound, one that cut through the snores. Ethan lay himself out prone on the ledge so as to present as low a profile possible to whatever might be coming their way. It couldn't possibly be the Boat Team, he could still see the women's lights bobbing way across the lake. He tossed a pebble over at Richard. It landed on his wrist and did the trick—with a last wheezing sound, he stopped snoring.

Just in time for a tremendously sized beast to come plodding out onto the ledge. Ethan could hardly believe his eyes.

The dinosaur was a massive four-legged beast, substantially larger than the largest elephant or rhino or water buffalo Ethan had ever seen. Four trunk-like legs with hooves the diameter of a small redwood tree. A long tail that came to a taper with no club or spiked weapon on the end of it. Most distinctive of all, an armored, bony collar at the base of the head, flaring out around the neck and tipped with bony knobs. A pair of pointy horns as long as Ethan was tall jutted from above the beast's eyes, and a single smaller horn sat atop its nostrils. The trio of horns gave the creature its name.

Triceratops.

Ethan couldn't help but notice the animal's mouth was oddly beak-like, as if the mouth of a giant squid had been fastened to the face of this monolithic reptile. The photographer shrunk back out of an abundance of caution. He could not imagine a more horrific fate than to be mauled to death by one of these primordial brutes. As he watched the triceratops, it dug its right front hoof into the ground, repeatedly sliding it across the same spot as if digging for something. It accompanied these efforts with grunts and snorts. Occasionally, it would dip its head down and employ one of its long tusks to assist in the digging.

Suddenly, the animal stopped its rooting around and lifted its gargantuan head while keeping its body still. Ethan found it amazing that such sheer bulk could be controlled so precisely. It stood stock still, eyes laser-focused on a spot in the distance. Ethan looked that way and didn't see anything. So what was the beast concerned with? A chill came over him as he was struck with a possibility. Had it detected the humans' scent? Or Richard's ragged breathing? If he started to snore again...

But in the next few seconds, that terrifying notion was dispelled when a second dinosaur—also an adult triceratops—rambled into sight, this one from the right side of the ledge near where Richard slept. The newcomer also halted suddenly upon sensing it was not alone. Not only was there another creature there, but one of its own kind. Although he'd never had the chance to observe dinosaurs in the wild before this fateful trip, Ethan knew that when two adult animals of the same species met, they were likely either one of two things: potential mates, or rivals. Which would these be? He certainly had no idea how to tell a male triceratops from a female at a distance.

But he didn't have long to wonder as both triceratops broke into a lumbering gallop toward each other.

Fight!

Ethan brought up his camera and hit the video button. He took more care than usual to verify it was actually recording. This was a once-in-a-lifetime event, and he wouldn't be able to live it down were he to find out later that he hadn't actually been recording, or that the battery had died or the memory card was full. But everything was in order, and so Ethan held the camera steady while he watched the action unfold.

It reminded him of two bighorn sheep he'd once observed ramming each other in the mountains of the Sonoran Desert in Arizona. Only this, of course, was on a much larger scale. Both animals ran headlong at full speed into each other, the sharp *crack* of their bony impact echoing off the sides of the volcanic lake.

Then, as with the sheep, they locked horns, twisting and turning their heads as they grappled for an advantage.

The triceratops Ethan had been watching before the challenger arrived was the first to go to its knees, employing its front legs to clinch its opponent while it knelt on its hind legs. Both dinosaurs roared as they did battle, each seeking to intimidate the other. What they were fighting over, whether mates or food or territory, Ethan didn't know. But whatever it was, he could plainly see that it was deadly serious. The newcomer gyrated its neck until it unlocked one of its tusks. With its newly freed weapon, the challenging triceratops swung its mighty head at its rival's neck, but the blow glanced off its foe's armored collar.

Ethan's triceratops (for some reason he silently rooted for the one he'd been watching first) pushed off of its opponent and countered with its own gore attack. It lowered its head and thrust its twin longhorns at its adversary's flank. The maneuver was successful, the right horn embedding almost its full length into its attacker's flesh, while the left sunk to within half its length. The gored triceratops brayed loudly and rolled over onto its right side, but the beast with the upper hand stayed with its quarry, moving forward to keep its formidable tusks buried in its opponent's flesh. It then placed its two front feet atop its fallen adversary's side, preventing it from rolling off the horns.

The gored triceratops lifted its head off the ground, shaking it to and fro to no avail. It could not reach its attacker. Then Ethan's charge reared back, pulling its horns from the other dinosaur's side with a wet sucking sound that made Ethan cringe. Then the standing mega-beast gored its opponent anew, this time in the lower abdomen. It shook its head violently in order to inflict massive damage. When it backed off, it left a gaping hole in the fallen creature's belly, spilling intestinal mass onto the charred rock.

In a final coup de grâce, Ethan's triceratops leapt onto its enemy's head and neck above the fringing armor, breaking its spine while simultaneously delivering a concussive blow to the skull as it smashed it into the rocky ground.

With a last gasp, the felled triceratops closed its eyes and was no more. The victorious animal threw its head back and vocalized a thunderous howl that told the island, *I have won.* Then the victor began to feed, ripping out chunks of its dead opponent's shoulder meat with its sharp beak and wolfing them down like a hungry dog with a raw steak.

Ethan slowly and silently retreated from the edge of his high hide, turning off the video. He shook his head at the ultimate fate of the defeated triceratops—resting in some dormant, hibernation state for untold millions of years only to be resurrected for a blink of an eye in order to fight and die.

The triumphant dinosaur apparently didn't like the taste of its own kind, for it stomped off in the direction from which it came before it had consumed much. When he was certain it was not returning, Ethan jumped down from his ledge. He looked over at Richard. Unbelievably, the explorer was still sound asleep, now beginning to snore again. Probably not a good sign. He'd heard somewhere that seriously injured people shouldn't be allowed to fall asleep, or was that only if they were in the freezing cold? It's a good thing the doctor was on the way over, he thought.

Ethan went to Richard and shook him gently by the shoulder. "Hey, you okay?"

The explorer took a long time to snap out of it, slowly awakening as if from a dream. "Yes, yes, quite all right," he said at length.

"Good. You missed one hell of a show while you were out. Take a look at—"

Before Ethan could finish his sentence, they felt the ground rumble beneath their feet. Rock began to tumble down from high above. Ethan froze with fear. *Not this. Not now...* But as the shaking continued, he knew it was real, it was happening.

Earthquake.

CHAPTER 16

"How much farther is it, Anita?" Skylar's voice carried more than a hint of frustration.

"Why are you asking me, anyway?" Anita swung her flashlight out into the lake as they walked, hoping she wouldn't spot their little raft adrift in the middle of the strange body of water, but at the same time knowing it was possible.

"You're the boat expert, you're in charge of the boat, that's why."

"You were there when we got out of the raft and left it there. Why don't you know where it is?"

"Ladies, please!" Lara tried to keep the peace. "We're all friends here. We need to stick—"

Lara, who had been walking along the narrow ledge with her left hand trailing along the wall so that she knew how much room she had, suddenly felt that wall move. She stopped walking to be sure she wasn't imagining things. The earth shook again, this time beneath her feet. Sheets of rock started to slide down the wall to their left, slamming into the lava shelf both in front of and behind them.

"Earthquake!" Skylar moved forward, toward where the raft was supposed to be, but froze in place when a slab of rock crashed a few feet in front of her. Lara made forward progress off to her right while Anita stood in place, screaming and crying.

Waves began breaking over the ledge, flooding it knee deep with a forceful rush of water that made it difficult to stand. Lara waved her light beam further out along the lake shore, maybe 25 more feet, where a cave entrance offered shelter from the falling debris. Or did it?

Lara yelled over to Skylar as more rocks exploded on the flooded ground around them, splashing them head to toe. "We could hang in the doorway of that cave!"

"What if it collapses in the quake?"

The ground shook violently, and all three of the expedition members lost their balance. "Chance we'll have to take. Not sure how long we'll last out here." Skylar and Lara started for the cave, but when they looked back, Anita wasn't following.

Lara called back to her. "Anita, come on—we'll be safer under there until it stops."

But the explorer stayed where she was, trembling as water swirled around her waist. Skylar made a move for Anita, to help her, deciding it was time to endear herself a little to the team. She eyed Lara as she dodged small pieces of shattering rock on her way to Anita.

"Keep going, check it out. I'll bring her there."

Lara nodded and ran to the cave entrance, where she stood under the natural arch opening watching the rocks fall outside. If a cave-in did happen, she would likely have time to run out before being buried under countless tons of lava rock. That's what she hoped, anyway.

Skylar arrived at the cave entrance with Anita in tow. The sailor seemed to have calmed down some and stood with her two colleagues as they stared out into a vision of Hell, of brimstone and fire and falling rock.

Part of the lake surface itself was ablaze, the water itself seeming to burn. Skylar speculated aloud it was excess sulfur gas igniting, but no one cared. More of the wall fell until it seemed like the entire volcano was coming down around them. They backed deeper into the cave to avoid the geological shrapnel of fragmenting rock. Skylar and Lara walked slowly, side by side, back into the cave, Anita right behind them. All three wore their headlamps while they swept hand-held lights around the walls of the cave.

Skylar directed her light beam up near the ceiling and watched, stunned, as one of the stony boulders fell to the ground and cracked, not ten feet in front of them.

"It's one of the cysts!" she warned.

And then another of the boulders loosed from the ceiling and dropped to the ground. This one didn't shatter or crack on impact, but was clearly wobbling under its own power long after it should have stopped moving from the fall.

"More of them are coming down!" Anita backed toward the cave entrance.

"I think the shaking is stopping." Skylar held out her arms, as though balancing on a beam. The ground no longer rolled beneath their feet, but outside the cave, they could still hear the sloshing of lake water as it swept over the ledge.

"It's cracking open. Let's go, c'mon!" Lara turned and ran toward the exit while Skylar continued to examine the ceiling, trying to figure out some geological quandary that would tell her if the collapse was over or not. But now she looked back at the cysts and knew she had bigger problems to worry about.

The first one that had dropped, also the largest, now had a dinosaur head poking out of it, and a tail, too. Anita tripped and fell but got to her feet quickly, running after Lara to the edge of the cave. Skylar turned away from the hatching lizard for a split second to see what was going on with Anita, and when she turned back around, she found herself laying eyes on a full-grown stegosaurus. It was unmistakable, an iconic dinosaur that an appreciable percentage of school-aged children would always be able to identify. The armor-like plates along the back, the spiked tail, the comparatively tiny head…

Skylar thought they were plant eaters, but still, it didn't much matter what they ate if a 7,000-pound animal trampled over you or whipped you with its spiky tail. Skylar, afraid to turn her back to the beast, walked backwards toward the cave exit while the stegosaurus shook off the remaining rock fragments. Then it started to walk away from its crumbled cyst, also toward the exit. Skylar watched as it sniffed the air, raising and lowering a head that seemed more apt to fit a large snake than a three-and-a-half-ton animal.

When it leveled out its head and began to charge, Skylar turned and ran, warning the others as she fled. "Move out of the way, it's coming!"

Lara and Anita peeled off to the left and right, respectively, outside the cave. Skylar came running through the middle, straight out of the cave toward the lake.

She saw the raft off to her left, hanging half off the rocky shelf. "I see the boat! C'mon!"

Lara started to run for the raft, but Anita still clung to the wall just outside the cave. Then the stegosaurus barreled out of the opening, skidding as its feet slipped on the wet rock shelf, its front legs splaying awkwardly until it recovered, slowing a bit but still running toward Lara and Skylar.

"Let's go, Anita!" Lara yelled behind her.

Skylar got to the raft first and kicked it over the ledge into the water, a three-foot drop. She heard Lara's boots pounding the rock shelf behind her. She could also pick up the dinosaur's heavy gait as it galloped after Lara, thundering toward the raft. Skylar was in a kind of mental auto-pilot, doing nothing other than carrying out direct physical actions needed to launch the boat.

She picked up the paddle and jumped into the raft.

"Wait for us, Skylar!" Lara sounded panicked, and Skylar knew she must be in order to level such an unspoken accusation at her. Did she really think she would leave two team members behind to be mauled by a prehistoric monster? *You stole those diamonds, doesn't that make you a bad person?* Skylar knew her conscience had chosen a terrible time to rear its ugly head, so she went into pure action mode again, paddling the boat so that it stayed butted up against the rocks, ready for the others to jump into.

Lara flew over the edge of the shelf and landed in the raft like a hyper kid jumping in a bounce house. Skylar reached out and kept her from bouncing out into the water, pulling her back down into the boat.

The stegosaurus slowed as it reached the edge of the shelf and swung its head out on its long neck until it passed over the raft. Skylar smashed it in the neck with the edge of the paddle. It snorted once and then reared up on its two hind legs, withdrawing its head and neck.

"Wait for me!" Anita appeared in the middle of the ledge, to the right of the dinosaur from Skylar's vantage point. Was she crazy, drawing attention to herself like that? Skylar had to shake her head, but Lara shouted, "Run, Anita!" She waved her arm in a rapid beckoning motion. "We need to go right now, c'mon, you can do it!"

Anita bolted. Where the sudden burst of physicality came from, neither Skylar nor Lara was sure, but there was no doubt that Anita suddenly looked like a track all-star as she tore across that wet ledge.

The stegosaurus, alerted by her sudden motion, also spurred itself into action. It lumbered toward her like a jerky locomotive. Anita kept her eyes focused straight ahead on the raft, not turning her head, while Skylar and Lara continued to urge her on.

"Jump, jump, jump!" Skylar paddled the boat a few feet out from the ledge so that the sprinter would be able to land in it after a flying leap from the ledge. That would also put them a little further from the charging dinosaur's reach.

Anita launched into a high jump that had her sailing through the air over the ledge. Skylar backed the boat out some more even as Anita traveled through the air. Lara shifted her body to the middle of the raft, aware that Anita was going to land at the front end where she had been seated.

The explorer hurtled into the raft with an *oomph*, propelling it further out into the lake with her momentum.

The dinosaur reached the edge of the shelf where Anita had jumped off, digging its feet into the rock to keep from sliding off the edge. Its right front leg slipped over, but it stopped itself in time. Then it stuck its head out over the water, raising and lowering it as though it might not be able to see the raft but was sniffing for its scent.

The three boaters watched as the animal turned around and walked back toward where the ledge met the inner wall of the volcano. At first, it looked like it was heading back inside the cave from where it had hatched, but then it stalked off to the right.

Skylar pointed. "Look, it's going for that opening there." A fissure that was tall and narrow glowed orange at its opening, no doubt containing still flowing rivers of lava inside. The women watched as the stegosaurus disappeared into that opening. Another minute passed and still it had not come back out.

"That looks like a newly created crevice. Wonder if it leads somewhere?" Skylar aimed her light at the fissure.

Lara saw a flashlight strobing on the other side of the lake and reminded them that they should get over to Boat Team and see how they had fared in the quake.

Anita held an arm out to Skylar. "I'll take the paddle now."

CHAPTER 17

"Damn it, where are they?" Richard deflected a volley of small stones from his face with an arm. The brunt of the earthquake had passed, but the rock around them was decidedly unstable. The novelty of the dead triceratops had worn off, as had the wow factor of having slept through two huge beasts fighting to the death, and now there was only concern for when the rest of their team would reach them.

"They're coming across now!" Ethan pointed out to the middle of the lake where a flashlight winked. Then the radio came to life with Lara's voice.

"We see you and we're coming for you. Hang tight."

"Do we have a choice?" Richard muttered. Ethan frowned at him and replied into the radio. "Copy that. Standing by."

Ethan could see that the earthquake had further soured Richard on their situation. And he couldn't exactly blame him. Ethan had entertained similar thoughts, but the difference was he kept them to himself. There was no need to damage morale in the already-fractured group. Richard was such a seasoned explorer, didn't he know that? He was about to say something about it—he wanted to put an end to the bickering before the Boat Team got here—when he heard scratching sounds coming from both right and left of them.

Not again! Richard feared the victorious triceratops was back, but then Richard got his attention.

"What is *that*?" Richard pointed at a bird-like animal, no more than two-feet high, that hopped into sight on the ground from their left. It possessed two legs like a bipedal reptile, but also had feathers that gave it a red and white striped appearance, while its leg skin was a drab shade of green.

"Looks like a cross between a bird and a lizard."

"Never seen anything like it. Why is it here? How is it here—this is a brand new island!"

Ethan looked at Richard. "They hatched out of those rocks, I guess, like the bigger ones." He indicated the dead triceratops in their midst.

"You mean, these little ones are dinosaurs, too?"

Ethan shrugged as a second one of the bird-like lizards hopped into view from the right side. It bumped chests with its fellow reptile and then the two of them ran around in quick circles while making clicking noises.

"Normally, I'd say no, but given that we just saw two triceratops, an ankylosaurus not too long before that, and some other aquatic one, too, I'm inclined to say yes, because we know dinosaurs are on this island. I have read that dinosaurs were probably more bird-like than we thought and that they had feathers, too."

"You're really annoying, you know that, Ethan? Is there anything you don't—?"

"Heads up, here comes more of them!" A veritable avalanche of the animals tumbled down from the cliff above, hitting the ground hard but seeming to suffer no ill effects, immediately churning around in circles with the first two individuals. Soon after, a group of them broke away and began eating the gored triceratops. Their crow-like beaks pecked stringy morsels of flesh from the slain giant while the two men wondered if the herd of predators would turn on them next.

Richard winced with the effort of reaching for the machete in his pack, only to remember with a flood of adrenaline that the last time he saw it, it was buried to the hilt in the velociraptor. But the machete was not his only blade. He swiped a fixed blade knife with a five-inch blade from a sheath attached to the outside of his pack. He managed to grip it and hold it in front of him just as one of the reptile-chickens launched itself at his chest. Richard hit the animal square in the neck with his blade, cutting the head off.

"How do you like me now, turkey?" Ethan glanced over at the explorer in time to see him throw his head back and cackle madly, clearly enjoying his kill way too much. Richard caught him staring and straightened up, asking Ethan, "Where are those girls, anyway?" He looked out across the lake.

But as much as Richard wanted to move on to the next problem at hand, the small dinosaurs still loitered around, and they were far from done. Not all of them were satisfied with gorging on the dead goliath, either. Six of them now launched themselves at Ethan. They hopped up into the air, flapping their wings a bit but not actually flying. The messy bird brigade swarmed around the photographer, their sharp beaks pecking at his legs. Even with jeans on, he could feel them drawing blood, and possibly infecting him with God knows what, maybe some prehistoric disease for which there could be no cure. *Great.*

"Richard, if you can move, I could use some help." Ethan grabbed one of the reptiles with both hands and gave it an overhead, double-armed catapult into the lake, where it fluttered its wings for a moment and then sank quickly out of sight.

"The little bastards can't swim! Chuck 'em into the lake if you can." Ethan soccer-kicked another one into the water, taking pleasure in feeling the creature's bones crack beneath his boot. Then, as he prepared to defend himself against another pint-sized attacker, the bird-thing's head exploded. Ethan saw a fist-sized hunk of rock come to rest on the ground next to the dead animal, and next he heard Richard whooping it up.

"Score!" After a few more similar volleys, the remaining animals scurried off out of sight along the ledge. By the time both of them checked their wounds, Richard saying his were insignificant compared to the ones he had already sustained, the raft was gliding up onto the rocky shore.

CHAPTER 18

Ethan grabbed a rope thrown by Anita and pulled the raft up onto the shore. The three women got out and looked around, more surprised to see only two people waiting for them than they were by the dead triceratops slopped on the ledge. Skylar, seeing that Richard was bad off, walked up to Ethan. "What happened here? It's just you two?" She eyed the three-horned behemoth doubtfully.

Ethan nodded solemnly before taking a deep breath. Then he recounted the grisly deaths of Kai, George, and the Tongan native, finishing with an account of Richard's injuries and the triceratops and chicken-dinos.

Skylar, in turn, relayed what happened to Joystna, finishing by looking away from the group with a gleam in her eye. They were worried about losing the doctor, but she was secretly glad to have lost George. Now that the other geologist was dead—the only other scientist on the expedition, period—Skylar's personal agenda just got a little easier. There was no one to challenge her geological descriptions now. She'd been concerned that if one of the team members mentioned that the glittering jewels embedded into the volcano were mica—a superficially glittery mineral but that also happened to be near worthless—that it would come back to haunt her. No need to worry about that now. By the time anyone asked about back in the States, it would be too late. She'd be gone with her diamonds.

Ethan's face fell with the implication that they'd lost Joystna. "Aye, tough break, losing our physician." Richard, who had been watching them converse, spoke up, his voice weak and phlegmy.

"Where's Joystna? You need to go back across to get her in a second trip? You could have put the doctor aboard first, you know." His body shook with a hacking, wet cough.

Ethan shook his head while walking toward Richard. "Joystna didn't make it."

Richard's eyes opened wide as he was stunned into silence with the grave ramifications. There would be no significant medical care for any of them until they got off the island.

Lara read his expression and told him how they'd divided the contents of Joystna's medical kit among them. Lara told him she'd take a look at his wounds, clean them up, and see what she could do. She gave him some antibiotics and pain pills, but Richard's mood continued to sour along with the blood that continued to seep out of him. He nodded to the satellite phone that could be seen clipped to Lara's pack where she'd left it on the ground.

"Have you gotten out with that yet?"

Lara shook her head. "No, tried several times, but we need a clear signal to the sky. We need to get topside. Now that our two teams are together…" She paused, looking around and seeing that the entire expedition now consisted of only five people. "…we can get up top and place that extraction call."

After a brief rest, they began loading their gear into the raft. Anita eyed the little boat dubiously. "It's only rated for four people max, and now we've got five plus lots of gear. We'll be overloaded, but if we go slow, we should be okay."

"I hope you're right." Richard pushed off the ledge he'd been sitting on with a grunt, standing on his own two feet. "Because believe me, you wouldn't want to swim around in that lake if you saw the thing that ate George." He shuddered visibly as though recalling the incident with the plesiosaur clearly in his mind's eye.

After reiterating that Ethan and Richard had fallen into the lake through the collapsed slope and therefore had not found a way down from above, Lara mentioned that there were a series of caves on the opposite shore. Seeing nothing promising on this side of the lake, and combined with the fact that a triceratops and herd of small dinosaurs roamed somewhere nearby, they decided to row back across the lake to explore those possibilities.

They carried Richard into the raft, gently easing him down to a laying position to reduce the strain on his newly dressed dinosaur wounds. Then the rest of them carefully boarded, Anita once again in charge of paddling. Ethan was last to board, and he took a final look at the massacred triceratops, which had started to smell as it rotted into the fetid, humid air. He looked at it closely and thought there was something odd about it. He couldn't place it at first but then it occurred to him: no bugs. How odd was it to see a rotting corpse in the wilderness that attracted no insects? Ethan had never seen it before, that was for sure. He had little doubt that if this carcass were to lay on an African savannah for all of ten minutes, it'd be crawling with bugs.

He climbed into the raft and gave them a shove off from shore. They glided out onto the vapor-shrouded surface of the lake. Ethan, Skylar and Lara shined their flashlights in all directions from the raft, searching both the shoreline for ways topside and the water itself for potential dangers including large sea creatures.

Even though the lake surface was calm and mostly smooth, the ripples from the earthquake waves having mostly subsided, the going was slow. After a time, they settled into a brooding silence. When at last they could see the opposite shore, Lara produced a pair of binoculars and began scoping out potential landing sites while Skylar shone the search beam. After scanning the area for about a minute, she zoomed in on a particular feature and fine-tuned the focus while Skylar held the light steady.

"There's a large cave opening, there." She pointed to a spot on shore while handing the binoculars off to the others, who took a look and passed them around.

"Looks plenty big, like it could lead somewhere." Ethan made eye contact with the others. "What do you think?"

They agreed to explore it, and Anita paddled the boat toward the new cave.

#

Once the raft had been safely brought up onto the rocky plateau that skirted the lake, the explorers made their way to the cave entrance. They entered five abreast, marveling at how wide the cave was. A cavern, really, except that the ceiling wasn't all that high, perhaps ten feet overhead. Around them, a series of gem-studded stalagmites shot up from the floor. They walked between them as they penetrated deeper into the cavern.

As they made their way deeper inside, the cavern narrowed until they could no longer walk side by side. Ethan took the lead, with the others walking two-by-two behind him.

"Doesn't look like this leads up, unfortunately." Ethan stooped as the ceiling lowered to barely above his head. He paced out a few more steps and then turned back to the others. "But it does lead somewhere—down. Let me see if I can get down there. I might be able to—whoa!"

Whatever it was he had viewed down below, it caused him to cut off what he was about to say in mid-sentence.

"What is it?" Skylar and the others clamored for a view of what lay beyond and below.

Ethan shook his head in wonderment before putting a finger to his lips and widening his eyes. Then he peered down once again on the incredible scene. A nest of dinosaurs—at least that's how Ethan thought of it, made of rocks. What little plant life had managed to grow so far on this brand new island was not nearly enough to line a nest, but the four-foot-high circular wall of rock was clearly intended to be a place for the mother to raise her young.

In the center of the nest, an adult two-legged dinosaur stood about twenty feet tall, its head reaching about to the level of Ethan in the tunnel, but about fifteen feet away. It superficially resembled a *T. rex*, its skin a pale greenish color. Maybe it was a *T. rex*? Ethan wasn't certain, but to him it looked more like… *What was that other one called?* He racked his brain to recall his childhood books.

Allosaurus! He mentally compared the long-ago images he'd seen in the books to the living, breathing beast right below him. *That's it! I'm looking at a mother allosaurus with her babies!* As the dinosaur reached its head down to the cavern floor and raised it again, this time bearing a hunk of meat, Ethan reached for his camera. His hands fumbled with excitement as he brought it to his eyes. He had just composed his image when he realized what the piece of meat was.

A human leg.

Dark-skinned, he knew it likely belonged to one of the Tongan party. His finger kept pressing the shutter button, but he had to look away from the scene as the four baby dinosaurs eagerly pulled at the carnivorous offering.

Suddenly, the allosaurus stopped moving. It froze, its head perfectly still but for the flaring of its nostrils. Ethan put a hand out for the others to be silent. Did it smell them? He didn't have long to wonder, for one second later, the allosaur leaped out of its nest, leaving its young to fight over the human leg.

It hopped once off the floor of the cavern, leaping at Ethan, who scrambled to turn and run with the others. But Anita blocked his path. She stood there transfixed, mesmerized by the oncoming monster, staring at it in a kind of bewildered rapture.

"Go, go!" Ethan urged, and she did, but a moment too late. The allosaurus jammed its oversized head into the ceiling over Ethan. He felt the rough, scaly skin of the underside of the reptile's chin scrape the back of his leg as he ran away. He gritted his teeth, expecting to feel the teeth bite into his leg next, and he pictured his own leg being ripped apart in the nest like the Tongan's. But the pain never came. Yet that in no way meant he was out of danger.

Up ahead, Ethan heard Anita cry out a split second before a slab of rock came crashing down from the ceiling, jarred loose by the dinosaur's head ram. He saw the others kneel down up ahead, and Ethan wondered why they would do that. Then he got to them and saw that Anita was pinned beneath the section of rock that had fallen. Behind them, the allosaur continued to growl and bash its head into the opening of the cave, no doubt seeking the prey inside.

Ethan watched the dinosaur for a few seconds to make sure it couldn't reach them. When he turned back to Anita, he expected her to be standing again, but she was still pinned beneath the fallen rock. "Come on, guys, help her up. We've got to go!"

As if to underscore Ethan's point, the allosaurus swung its wrecking ball of a head into the wall of the cave opening and knocked out a sizable hunk, making the entrance a little wider for it. "C'mon already, before it knocks enough wall down to fit its head back here!"

"We need a shovel." This from Lara, who shook her head at the impossibility of lifting the hunk of rock off of Anita.

"Skylar's got the only shovel."

They all looked to the geologist, and she hesitated for a moment, as if unsure about something.

"Skylar, come on!" Ethan urged.

Then she knelt down to her pack and produced a rock hammer, a stout tool, but nowhere near the length of a shovel.

"We need that shovel, Skylar!" Ethan couldn't hide the exasperation in his voice. The allosaur still rampaged at the entrance, breaking away the tunnel piece by crashing piece.

"I don't have it."

"What do you mean you don't have it?" Ethan spoke over Anita's yelps of pain as they moved the rock little by precious little over her trapped leg.

"I'm sorry, but it seems I forgot to put it back in my pack after one of our rest stops."

"Just give us the hammer, then!" Lara held out her two hands, willing her to toss it to her. She went to work on the rock while the allosaurus went to work on its own rock at the entrance to the tunnel.

With Richard nearly incapacitated, the going was much slower than any of them preferred, especially Anita. But Lara managed to make progress, chipping away at the slab of rock pinning down the explorer. Still, the dinosaur's head reached further and further inside the tunnel-like passage with each passing minute. When its jaws snapped only a foot from Anita's torso, everyone else having moved to the other side of the rock that pinned her, the handle of the rock hammer cracked in half.

Anita's eyes bugged out as she saw it happen. "Fix it! Get another one! Do something, please! Don't let that thing eat me, whatever you do, please don't let it eat me!"

Ethan's gaze roved around the group. "Who's got another rock hammer, anything?" Everyone either replied in the negative or else bent down and searched through their backpacks. Time was not going to permit that, however, with the allosaurus now thrashing the base of its thick tail against the entrance of the cave, further loosening the rock and allowing its head to penetrate even farther inside, only inches from Anita's trapped body.

Ethan picked up a chunk of rock that had split off from the slab and used it as a crude hammer to break away the remaining pieces trapping Anita. Lara also picked up a rock and did the same, and just as the big lizard's scaly snout thrust forward, they snatched Anita out from under the pile of rubble. The creature's jaws snapped at the heap of broken rock while the group rushed back toward the main cavern.

When they got to within sight of the entrance, Ethan stopped and looked back toward the chamber containing the nest to see if the allosaurus was still in pursuit, if it had somehow made it through the tunnel. But either it could not fit, or had decided the humans no longer posed a threat to its young and so abandoned the pursuit.

"Come on, Ethan, let's get out of here." Richard's voice sounded weaker, no doubt as a result of the excitement and exertion. He fell into step with the others, and they exited the cave the same way they entered.

"I'm glad we made it out of there okay," Ethan said on exiting while looking out on the lake, "but we're still no closer to finding a way topside. Where should we try next?"

"Let's get back in the boat," Lara said, and they piled into it.

Anita paddled them out a little ways so that they had a good view of the shoreline. Skylar pointed to their left, along the rocky shelf fronting the lake. "We're not too far from where we ran from the stegosaurus into the raft. It ran into that narrow opening, there."

Lara nodded. "If that dinosaur fit back through there, the cave must be pretty big. It's tall, too." She looked up at the volcano's interior, the distant cone of light at the top at once mocking and beckoning them.

"Might as well try it," Ethan said. "I see other, smaller caves besides that one, too, if it turns out to be a dead end. Hopefully, they're not all full of allosaurus nests."

Anita rowed the raft near to the same spot they had launched from while the others kept a sharp lookout for predators. Lara stared into the fissure with binoculars and reported no sign of the behemoth.

Anita brought the boat up to the ledge and Ethan jumped out. He held the raft in place with a rope while the gear was handed out and everyone climbed up on shore. Richard was helped out by

Skylar and Ethan, moaning softly but not complaining about anything for the time being.

"What about the raft?" Anita eyed their craft now abandoned on the edge of the shelf. "Should we fold it up and take it with us in case we need it?"

This was met with a round of groans. After already taking on increased loads due to the medical kit, the last thing anyone looked forward to was carrying more stuff. But the boat did provide utility that only it could provide.

"Let's leave it here, but make sure it doesn't go anywhere." Ethan grabbed the rope and dragged the raft further from the edge, then picked up a medium-sized stone and set it inside the flimsy boat to weight it down. No one had any objections, and so they trekked across the ledge to the fissure.

Its jagged, oblong outline glowed orange as the team, with Skylar in the lead, entered the volcano's innards.

CHAPTER 19

"Stay in the middle." Skylar's warning was hardly necessary. On both sides of what was essentially a narrow gorge, with natural light filtering in from high above, rivers of lava flowed toward the lake. They hadn't seen them emptying into the lake, but Skylar said they must drain to it beneath the rock ledges.

As forbidding as the place was, the fact that they could see the outside, albeit very far above, had an uplifting effect on their spirits. Lara even tried the satellite phone, although as expected, that did not work. Further adding to their positivity was the lack of dinosaurs, at least so far. As Skylar plodded along, it was almost as though she were on just another field hike in some remote location, doing science. The heavy weight of her pack, laden with diamonds, further buoyed her temperament while at the same time tormenting her muscles.

The natural path they followed into the fissure gradually sloped upward the deeper inside they trekked. At first, the change was almost imperceptible, but after a while, Ethan stood in one place and looked back toward the exit. It was no longer visible because they had risen in elevation and no longer had a direct line of sight with it. He turned back around and saw that the trail in front of them—as rocky and perilous as it may be—continued upward, and at an even steeper angle.

"Guys, I don't want to speak too soon, but I think we may have found a winner with this cavern."

"Long way to go." Skylar didn't bother turning around, she just kept marching up the fissure as though physically drawn to the light at the top.

The going up the trail was steady, but slow enough that even Richard had little trouble keeping up. Having to stop to walk around a boulder—they walked *very* carefully around boulders—or jump across a break in the ground where bright red lava bubbled below—meant that he was able to keep up, for it was long stretches of open ground where he would show his weakness, and of those there were none.

After a time the conversation dropped to a functional minimum ("watch out for that crack," or "pass me the binoculars, will you?"), the sound of occasional falling rock punctuating the silence. Thoughts of rescue kept the group plodding onward, and they took the path further up into the fissure.

Skylar, still in the lead, saw a few hints of the diamond riches that lay just below the surface layer of rock, but of course, she could do nothing about it in such close proximity to the others and so turned her thoughts to other matters. Such as the stegosaurus. It wasn't lost on her that, although the path was narrow, the dinosaur *could* still be in here somewhere. They hadn't seen it leave, after all, although it could have exited the fissure while they were taking the boat back across the lake to pick up Richard and Ethan.

If it hadn't exited, though… Skylar looked away from the sparkle of a particularly large stone high on the wall. If it hadn't exited, that was both a good and a bad thing. Good, because it meant this passage actually led somewhere for quite a ways, but bad, obviously because it meant they could have to contend with the beast once again. By the time Skylar broke from these thoughts, she saw that the landscape was changing. The slope became very steep while at the same time curving off to the left.

Skylar followed the trail, warning the group that the ceiling was becoming lower. And then the passage they had been following since they entered the fissure came to an abrupt end. Well, not an end, exactly, Skylar thought as she stopped walking. But certainly a drastic change.

Tendrils of mist wafted up from below, shrouding the entrance to what appeared to be a tunnel set into the side of the volcano. She noted that she would have to duck to fit inside the tunnel, meaning there was no way the stegosaurus could have made it. She shrugged to herself while waiting for the others to catch up.

She looked down into the fissure to see if she could sight the stegosaurus, but there was only a lava river far below. If the dinosaur had fallen down this way, there would likely be no trace of it. Then, just as she was about to avert her gaze back to the tunnel, her peripheral vision caught a glittering fount of light off to her left. About two feet down over the ledge protruded a massive hunk of raw diamond so brilliant it almost looked as though it had already been polished. And perhaps it had been, she thought, polished by natural geological processes during the volcano's formation.

But Skylar's interest in geology at this point was not scientific. She heard Richard groan in pain while the others came to his assistance, still a little ways back on the path. Quickly, she shrugged off her already heavy pack and took from it her rock hammer. She lay down on the trail so that her arms dangled over the side where the gemstone was. *Imagine if I can get this one...no more after this, I'll be so set for life...*

She tried to be as quiet as possible with the hammer, hoping that if it was heard it would be passed off as typical boots kicking rocks out of the way. Still, a certain amount of racket was inevitable, and to Skylar's ears, the echoing of the tool's blows seemed to announce to the entire island, "Diamond thief here!"

When the stone was loose, she gripped the base of it with one hand gave it a final blow with the hammer, which broke it loose. A small chunk of diamond, perhaps three karats' worth, dropped away from the larger mass and plummeted to the lava below, while the rest of the glorious gem came free in her gloved hand, a fist-sized lump.

Skylar heard the footsteps of the others approaching and quickly dragged herself back onto the path. She pulled her pack to her and thrust the hand with the rock inside, as though she were looking for something.

"Something down there?" Richard's gaze traveled over the edge of the path.

Skylar shook her head. "No, I was just taking a look to see if I could learn something more about the geology of this place, maybe see if there might be ways that the stegosaurus could have gone down there, too."

"Because he didn't fit through that tunnel, I guess?" This from Ethan, who shone his light beam into the confined passage.

Skylar got to her feet and dusted off her pants. "Exactly. So where did it go?"

Before anyone could answer, Ethan stepped into the tunnel, stooping to duck under the entrance lip. The others huddled at the entrance and waited until he had penetrated some distance inside, calling back that, "Looks like it leads somewhere." At that, the rest of them entered the tunnel, Richard requiring assistance from the others to walk because it aggravated his injuries to bend over in order to fit beneath the ceiling.

They slogged on until they caught up with Ethan, who was grinning ear to ear, his flashlight off. "Turn your lights off." One by one, the flashlights were doused until they stood bathed in what he wanted them to see: natural light flooding in from above.

"I think it's safe to say this lets out to the outside." He finished by flicking his light back on in preparation for the remaining trek out of the tunnel. The optimism was infectious and the group experienced renewed energy as they hunched their way toward the sunlight. The incline became steeper the further they went, until when they were very near the tunnel's exit, they had to crawl the final few feet.

Ethan and Skylar belly-crawled to the edge of the tunnel first, scrambling for their sunglasses as their eyes were met with tropical sunshine and bright blue sky after the dim confines of caves and tunnels. Ethan stuck his head out into the air and looked around.

"Oh my God, will you look at this!"

CHAPTER 20

"How can we look at anything but your two asses with you blocking the view like that?" Richard grumbled.

But nothing could spoil Ethan's good mood. "I certainly hope it's not my ass you're looking at as long as this lovely lady is lying here next to me."

The group laughed, for the first time in a long time, while Ethan and Skylar crawled out of the tunnel onto a cramped platform cut into the volcano's outer slope.

"We're a little more than halfway up, from the looks of things." Ethan stood up fully for the first time since entering the tunnel. He stretched, taking in the magnificent view of the empty Pacific Ocean and the brown volcano dropping precariously to meet it.

Skylar looked higher, at where there was to go from here. "Doesn't look easy to get to, but I see what looks like a small plateau maybe forty feet above us, where we could set up a staging area and probably make that sat-phone call."

Ethan rubbed the stubble on his chin as he pondered the proposed route. "That's a near vertical stretch. We'll have to break out the climbing gear, hammer in some pitons…"

Skylar looked past Ethan to the rest of the group. "Lara, can you get a signal from the edge here?"

The others parted to make way for the communications tech to move to the opening in the volcano's face. Skylar stepped back into the tunnel, and Lara took her place at the window to the sky. She activated the sat-phone and stared at its screen while waiting to see if it would acquire a signal. A minute passed. and she shook her head.

"It still says 'need clear view of sky'."

Ethan shrugged. "We'll have to make the climb, then. Even if we did make contact from here, there's no way a heli could pick us up from this tunnel, anyway. So we might as well get on with it."

Each of them set up their climbing gear. Richard was the most experienced climber of them, but due to his injuries, they decided Ethan should be the lead climber. The lead was the riskiest job, since he was the one who had to place the first safety lines, which the others would make use of as they followed in his vertical footsteps. It was crucial, therefore, that this person be extremely skilled, and Ethan's experience climbing in the Alps to photograph eagles' nests had earned him worldwide recognition as a wildlife photographer.

Ethan finished setting up his gear and asked Anita to belay him. She was also a somewhat experienced climber, and used to working with ropes and knots as a sailor. Furthermore, she was physically stronger than Lara and Skylar, and Ethan wanted someone with strength if he had to depend on them to catch him in a fall.

He moved to the edge and hammered a piton—a metal spike used to hold a rope—into the rock. The blows from his piton hammer echoed off the volcanic slope as Ethan drove the spike home. He clipped a rope to his climbing harness and ran it through the piton. Anita held the other end of the rope, ready to tighten it down should Ethan fall, but letting out slack as he climbed.

He began his ascent by placing a foot on an obvious hold, then reaching with his right arm for another one seven feet up. He found there to be sufficient holds, and the porous lava rock, although rough on his hands, even with climbing gloves on, made for a good grip. It could still crumble, though, and this was a constant concern as he made his ascent. When he had gone about fifteen feet up, Ethan rigged another piton with a safety rope so that, should he fall, he would be caught from this point instead of fifteen feet below at the tunnel.

He continued his ascent through the most vertical section of the wall, placing each foot and hand with great care. He drove home one more piton on the way up the face, then was able to climb the rest of the way, throwing an arm over the edge of the plateau and lifting himself up and over onto the flat piece of hard ground.

"Made it! Plenty of room up here for everybody." He hammered in a piton at the edge of the platform and then dropped a rope down to the group. "Who's up next?"

"Have Lara go next," Richard called up. "She's got the sat-phone and we need to place that call."

"Feel up to it, Lara?" Ethan called down.

She tightened down the straps on her backpack and stepped up to the rope while Anita assisted her with the climbing harness. "Here goes nothing."

Lara put a foot in the same hold Ethan had used, and started up the wall.

"You go, girl, you can do it!" Anita cheered.

The others also gave shouts of encouragement, the mood lightening somewhat as they anticipated help being summoned within minutes. Lara climbed with efficiency and grace, reaching the halfway point of the face only a little after Ethan had done it. Her right foot slipped when she pushed off a micro-ledge in the wall, and she fell. Fortunately, she was only a few feet higher than the nearest safety line and so she didn't have far to drop. A scraped wrist and a bruised knee later, she was back on the upward move, scaling the wall as if nothing had happened.

When Lara was about two-thirds of the way up, Skylar heard a noise in the air, somewhere outside the tunnel. She told the others to hush and stared out at the sky over the ocean, listening over Lara's climbing efforts.

Richard looked at her with a *well, what?* expression. But suddenly, an explanation was no longer required, because at that moment, the screeching noise became louder, much louder. Looking down and to their left, they could see something, too.

"There! It's coming! Pterodactyl!" The group hadn't heard Skylar panic before, but after what she had seen happen to Joystna, she became more than a little uneasy at the sight of another winged reptile coming to torment them.

Lara froze on the wall like the proverbial deer in headlights. This time, though, she was the deer, and she knew it.

"Move, Lara! Go!" Ethan yelled down to her as he spotted the ptero slanting up toward Lara's rock wall from below. "Up!" He added that, because for all he knew, she might think it was faster to slide down the safety line to the tunnel exit on the side of the volcano.

She climbed, up and to the right, connecting with solid hand- and foot-holds on her way to Ethan.

But the airborne mega-predator suddenly shifted direction with a squawk. It came now straight on for the tunnel. Skylar stumbled backwards, knocking into Richard, who howled like a banshee, clutching at his bandaged mid-section as he rolled back into the tunnel. Pain aside, Skylar's move probably saved his life. The massive pterodactyl—Skylar swore it was twice as large as the one that took Joystna—dove into the tunnel. Richard and Skylar, tangled up on the floor of the tunnel, were low enough to be safe. The organic spear of the ptero's closed beak jabbed through the air above their heads.

Anita barely missed the weapon by staying on her feet and running away from the exit as fast as her stooped position would permit. The ptero needed its wings at least partway unfurled to maintain balance, and its wingspan was too great to allow it to penetrate any deeper into the tunnel. The animal backed out of the cave, wildly hissing and tossing its head. When it reached the opening, it pushed off in what looked like an awkward move, but like a cat that manages to land on its feet, the ptero rolled until it unfurled its wings until it flew in a graceful arc.

This new flight path took it back toward the wall, where Lara was one handhold away from being able to grab Ethan's strong, outstretched arm. Ethan locked eyes with her and tried to keep the fear out of his voice. "Come to me, Lara. Just one more hold. You can do it…"

Ethan lay flat on the plateau, leaning over, but even so, he risked being attacked by the flying marauder by exposing himself like that rather than taking cover behind a group of rocks further back on the plateau.

Lara didn't turn around to look, but she could hear the hideous shrieking the thing made as it neared. She swore, whether imagined or not, that she could feel a rush of air as the ptero approached. Felt the panic envelop her senses, prevent her from thinking so that all she wanted to do was act. The communications specialist jumped for that next hold, the one that would allow her to connect with Ethan...

Her left foot landed on the tiny outcropping of rock. The move was not one of her best, that was for sure. It was reckless, ungainly, and born of desperation, but it had worked and she would take it.

And then the pterodactyl took her, swiping her entire body from the cliff face with beak agape. Ethan almost threw himself over the edge of the plateau trying to grab Lara, whose fingertip brushed against his—it was that close. The terrifying reality that was the rest of Lara Cantrel's life unfolded with blinding speed as the ptero wheeled about in a circle. It passed close to the volcano's outer wall before swerving away at the last second.

This maneuver allowed the ptero to miss the wall, but its prey was not so lucky. Lara's head was smashed into the rock with alarming force, the sound of her skull cracking echoing off the lava facade. Ethan watched as the lizard-bird flew past him, its wing just out of reach as though taunting him. He saw Lara's broken face, mouth moving as if she tried to speak but no sound came out, only blood.

Then she was gone, carried by the volcanic monster out over the ocean.

The others had moved back to the tunnel exit, and now they watched in stupefied horror as their expedition-mate was dropped headlong into the Pacific, at least a hundred feet below. The pterodactyl hovered in the air, wings fully outstretched as it rode the updrafts. Then it dive-bombed, like a pelican knifing into the water after a fish. Only the fish was Lara.

Ethan watched her body float far below. It looked motionless but was far enough away that he couldn't be sure. He didn't give her good odds of surviving that ten-story fall, though, especially after the gruesome head injury. He was sure she was dead by now.

He hoped so, anyway, because next the ptero plunged into Lara, the beak opening around the human's neck and closing around it as it shot into the depths like a high diver into a pool. It took about thirty seconds for the ptero to emerge from the ocean. When it did, Ethan and the others were mortified to see that it had snapped off their associate's head while underwater.

The ptero now carried only the human head in its mouth as it skimmed low over the waves around the volcano's base.

CHAPTER 21

Ethan watched the pterodactyl fly out of sight somewhere around the curve of the volcano. He turned to the rest of the team—Skylar, Richard, and Anita, gawking at the departing predator from the hole in the side of the volcano.

"Make the climb now!"

Understandably, the trio of explorers were hesitant to leave the shelter of the tunnel. But with a little more goading, Ethan convinced them to make the move. With Anita and Skylar assisting Richard where necessary, and Ethan helping by pulling them up with a rope, the three of them managed to ascend to the plateau without incident, although the climb was fraught with tension as they constantly looked over their shoulders. Would the pterodactyl return? How many more of the winged beasts lurked around the island?

The entire expedition united once again, now whittled down to four people, Ethan scanned the skies for signs of pterodactyls while they discussed their options.

"So we lost our comm tech, and with her, all of her gear including the sat-phone." Skylar looked to Richard. "But each sub–team had one, right? So we can use yours to place our extraction call. If you still have it." She eyed him expectantly, aware that Slope Team had already lost half of its members.

Richard and Ethan exchanged awkward glances, recalling the chaotic scene at the volcano's summit with the marauding ankylosaurus, before they fell through to the lake. Richard picked at a crusty part of one of his bandages, slowly shaking his head.

"Which one of you had the other sat-phone?" Skylar demanded. Anita looked on, exhausted, scared, watching the exchange that would determine her fate.

"I did." Ethan pointed up to the summit. "I dropped it when the ground opened up after the first dinosaur hatched. But listen…" He paused while gathering his thoughts, Skylar and the others giving him their full attention. Ethan's face brightened after a moment's reflection.

"The last I saw it, it was resting a few feet down in a crevice. Just out of reach. With the dinosaur chasing me and the ground falling in, I couldn't stop to get it."

Skylar wrinkled her brow. "But did it fall through into the lake?"

Ethan shook his head. "I don't think it did, because the part that fell in was in front of me, and I remember the phone being behind me."

Richard nodded his agreement. "I never actually saw it, but from my vantage point, Ethan was running away from me with respect to where the dinosaur hatched from, I know that."

Skylar found this to be inconclusive, but shrugged while looking at the others. "If that's our only other phone, I suppose it's worth a look to get up there, if we can, and see if it's still there?"

"And if it still works—if it hasn't been cracked into pieces or burned up or something," Anita said dejectedly.

"We've got to try," Richard said.

"Let's take a short rest, eat something, get hydrated, then we'll make an attempt on the summit." Ethan delved into his bag and pulled out a packet of beef jerky. The others shrugged off their packs and set about having a quick lunch. The four of them were spread out around the small plateau, which was not perfectly flat but dotted with rocks here and there. Ethan and Skylar discussed possible routes to the summit based on what they could see from here, while Anita and Richard ate and drank in brooding silence.

After a time, Ethan saw Richard get up and walk behind a clump of rocks. It reminded him that he needed to urinate, and so he figured Richard must have found a good spot for that.

Ethan skirted around the left side of a boulder field, mentally deciding that right after this they needed to get moving. The trek to the summit would not be easy if doable at all. He wondered to himself what they would do if they couldn't all make it to the top—if they couldn't get that sat-phone. I'll probably just have to make a solo free climb ascent, he was thinking, when he saw Richard and stopped dead in his tracks.

The professional explorer jammed a collapsible tent pole in between two lava rocks so that it stuck there, straight up. *He's not taking a leak, so what's he doing?* Ethan shrank back behind a boulder while he observed Richard. He heard Anita and Skylar strike up a conversation in the background, but he tuned it out in order to stay focused on what Richard was doing.

The Brit now held a piece of fabric in his hands, and as Ethan watched, he unfurled it to reveal a flag of some kind. Then Richard threaded the flag over the tent pole, and Ethan saw that it was the Tongan national flag. *What in the Hell was going on here?*

"Excuse me, Richard?"

The explorer jumped at the words, startled at having been seen by someone obviously so close by. His face reddened as he turned away from the flag.

"I—well, you're excused, my dear boy. Just give a chap some privacy, would you? I would have gone over to the edge to take care of my business, but I figure the edge is not a safe place, what with what happened to Lara and all…"

"Cut the crap, Richard. What are you doing?" Ethan pointed to the flag. "What's the meaning of this?"

Richard gazed at the flag with a look of surprise. "Right, it looks like I found more evidence of the Tongans."

"*Richard!* Stop it. I saw you set that up yourself and put it there. Now you tell me what the hell is going on?"

"I told you—"

One of the boulders shielding Richard's activity from the rest of the group started to wobble. Ethan noticed it because of the way he was facing, but Richard continued stammering out a reply, oblivious.

"Richard, it's hatching, watch out!"

CHAPTER 22

Nuku'alofa, Tonga

CIA Special Agent Valea Esau wasn't looking forward to meeting with the King of Tonga again, but he had to warn him. He enjoyed a good working relationship with the political leader and wanted to keep it that way because it made his own job a lot easier. He stepped off the bus, one stop later than the one he'd used last time, so as to avoid being too repetitive. He opted not to take his own vehicle on these liaisons since he could be identified that way, and private vehicles were easier to follow than an individual switching between different modes of public transportation with no regular schedule.

As before, Valea was vetted by the gate guards and escorted up to the king's suite, where the booming voice told him to come in. Once the doors were closed, King Nau smiled and once again gravitated to his wet bar.

"What, you can't take anything I've got to say without a shot of liquor?" Valea smiled. He was all too aware that his very presence made a lot of people nervous by simple virtue of who he worked for, and His Royal Majesty Malo Nau was no exception.

"You know me by now, Valea. I like to at least pretend that you and I can have a good time while we conduct our affairs. What would you like? How about a glass of Tonga's finest rum?"

Valea didn't feel much like partaking, but he also knew that keeping things as pleasant as possible with the king was important, so he accepted the offer and took a seat at the coffee table. It took a fair amount of restraint not to blurt out what he came here to say, but his field experience told him to be patient. The king also took a seat, and after the two had clinked glasses, Valea got down to business.

"Your Majesty, I'm afraid my visit today does not bring good news."

"I presume this is about the expedition? I have heard nothing."

Valea nodded. "Unfortunately, not only have I not heard from our man on Expedition Gaia, but the U.N. has been out of contact with the entire team since they were dropped off, other than the air crew returning. The airmen did report a successful drop-off, that's all we know."

"How would they be in contact? I know our people do not have cellular reception there."

"Satellite phones." Valea leaned forward on the edge of his seat. "But not only that, Malo, we've done satellite imaging passovers and none of the party were sighted. So they must be underground in the volcano, is what we're thinking…"

"Wait…you look down on our country from space?"

Valea exhaled heavily. This was not what he wanted to get into. He held out a hand in a placating gesture. "Yes, your majesty, we looked down on the new island only."

The king's eyes narrowed. "I guess I will have to take your word on that."

"That's what this is all about, Malo. We want that new island, that's why we made it, remember? We're not reading the labels on your rum bottles or peeping in on your women."

The king knocked back his drink and set the glass down on the table with a *clack* and a crooked grin. "Please, do not worry. Go on."

Valea nodded. The king must want that revenue from having a U.S. military base on the new island very much indeed. Yet the steps to make that happen were complex and far from a sure thing. Valea needed to make this clear to the king. "Not all of this is within my control, your majesty. I want you to understand that."

"Of course. Please, tell me what it is you have come to say. Is everything all right?"

Valea stared down at the backs of his hands while he talked. "As I said, we've been out of contact with the team for a few days."

"Yes…"

"What I need to tell you, your majesty…" Valea looked up and made eye contact with him now. "…is that there is a contingency plan in place in the event that we do not hear from the team or should we learn that they are confirmed either missing or killed."

"And what is this contingency plan of which you speak?"

Valea took a long pull of his drink before setting it back on the table. "The plan is to extensively bomb the island until it falls back into the sea, and then to disavow all traces of the project known as Neptune's Inferno."

The king's mouth dropped open and his eyes grew wide. He stood from his chair, muscles tense. "What?! And destroy my kingdom's newest island?"

"We don't want to, your majesty. It's only as a last resort."

"But why? Why go through all of the trouble to create a new isle, only to blast it apart?"

"The orders come from much higher than my pay grade, Malo. But it has to do with not wanting the island to fall into the hands of another nation besides Tonga, because the U.S. is concerned that those countries would allow enemies of America to build military installations there."

"So if we can't have it, nobody can, is that it?"

Valea nodded. "Close enough. The reason I'm telling you this, Malo, is to make sure to keep all boat traffic out of the area. Military, fishing, recreational—it's not a safe place to be right now."

"I will make certain the area is kept clear. But I ask you, Valea, if the island is destroyed…" He hesitated, as if unsure of how to phrase his next thought.

"If it's destroyed, what?"

"That option was not presented to me during our initial agreement. What I agreed to was to allow you to…'artificially induce,' I believe your words were, the creation of a new island, which if successful, would result in the revenue stream for allowing your country to use it as a base of operations."

"I'm well aware of what the terms of the agreement were, King Nau. What is your point?"

"If the island is blown up, I believe the people of Tonga should be compensated for the inconvenience of the whole matter, in the form of a fee."

Valea rolled his eyes and took a deep breath. "Fine, that should be doable, should this come to pass. Remember, it might not. Hopefully, our team is alive and well."

CHAPTER 23

"Something's coming out of there! Move out of the way!" Ethan marveled at the creature emerging from the rock cyst while Richard stumbled to get past him. This animal was definitely a dinosaur, but not one that Ethan recognized. About the size of an adult African elephant and also with four legs, the reptile was a dull gray in color with the exception of a red, fleshy waddle on the crest of its head.

Ethan acted while the creature still extricated itself from its hibernation pod or whatever the stone was. He wedged himself sideways into a depression between two rocks, clearing the way for Richard to move back out to the main part of the plateau and the others.

The dinosaur—Ethan thought it might be of a type known as hadrosaur, but he really had no idea—shook off the last remnants of its casing and set about exploring its new world.

Richard ran out of the protective cover of the rocks, even though their maze-like closeness kept the beast from maneuvering well. The massive quadruped stormed right by Ethan, its tiny, bead-like eyes taking no notice of the human hiding in its midst.

The hadrosaur rocked back on its two hind legs and put its front legs up on a rock. Its mighty head swung back and forth as it looked over at the flat expanse of the plateau. It sprung off the ground with its hind legs, teetered on the rock and then landed on the other side…just as Richard came running out of the rocks across the plateau.

The injured explorer swiveled his head to the right as he ran, eyes widening in terror as he saw the mega-beast launch into a run toward him. Flat, open ground surrounded him now, and even Anita and Skylar, at the opposite end of the plateau, shrank back in fear behind a cluster of jagged lava rocks.

The hadrosaur had no trouble catching up to Richard, who tripped before the animal reached him. The man who had famously turned thirty years old while standing atop the summit of Mount Everest was splayed out on the ground of the newly minted volcano. He tensed himself for what he knew was coming. The dinosaur trampled him viciously, running over him, breaking his left arm with its left front foot while cracking his right femur with its right rear foot.

Richard's cry of agony was cut short when the monster's right front foot punched down on the human's head, grinding all of it into a sticky, pulpy goop on the hard lava rock ground, cutting short the memories of Richard's life flashing by. The beast made no effort to consume its victim, though. It walked away from the dead person, toward the other two humans.

"Ethan, where are you?" Skylar called from where she and Anita hid behind a rock. Had Ethan been trampled by this beast, too?

"Over here!" The photographer walked out from where he and Richard had been. He egged the creature on. "Hey, hey, right here, dinosaur! Hey!"

The creature turned around in a slow lumbering maneuver. Ethan knew the beast was incapable of stopping on a dime, such was the momentum its great bulk produced. He would use that to his advantage. Like a bullfighter teasing a mad bull, Ethan stood with his back to the edge of the plateau's cliff that he had ascended to get here.

"Hey dino…hey, c'mon, come get me!"

The dinosaur charged. It rumbled across the plateau, snorting along in a one-animal stampede. Ethan rocked back and forth on his toes, knowing he needed to be at the height of his agility to pull this off. At the last moment, when the hadrosaur lowered its great head in anticipation of ramming its target, Ethan feigned left and dodged right. The rampaging reptile swiped its head to the right, the fleshy waddle bobbing around, but its bulky mass had already been set into motion and would take more distance than it had in front of it to stop.

The barreling behemoth snorted as it ran headlong off the cliff, its tons of deadweight plunging to the bottom and breaking its neck on impact.

Cautiously, Ethan walked to the edge and looked down. He raised his arms in triumph as the two women began to clap. He had done it! Ethan Jones, killer of dinosaurs, had slain the beast. But his exultation was short-lived, for lying not far away was the crumpled remains of Richard Eavesley, renowned National Geographic Explorer-In-Residence. He moved to the body, knelt down and felt for a pulse even though having no head to speak of should mean certain death. Nevertheless, he went through the motions, grimacing as the arm bent at the most unnatural of angles when he picked up the wrist to place two fingers over the artery.

As expected, he felt only stillness. "He's gone," he added for finality, but he knew the words weren't needed.

Ethan walked to Skylar and Anita, who both sat on the ground, weary, miserable, looks of defeat beginning to take hold. It was just the three of them now, and Ethan knew it didn't take a statistician to see that with a starting group of eight, their odds for survival weren't good. Especially given the fact that they currently had no way to contact anyone for help. Ethan made eye contact with Skylar and Anita in turn. Of the two of them, Anita by far appeared the most shaken. She was sullen, not talking much lately, and beginning to retreat into her shell. Ethan had seen it before, during tribal warfare outbreaks in Africa when his nature photography team was caught in the crossfire, videoing piles of elephant ivory burning in bonfires set by the government to discourage poaching.

He knew from experience that any bright spot, no matter how weakly it shone, should be seized upon to provide hope and lift morale. He pointed to Richard's backpack, still sitting on the ground where he'd dumped it upon arrival for what was supposed to be a lunch break.

"Let's see what useful gear he has and divide it amongst us. Then we'll make our way to the summit and see about finding that sat-phone. Sound like a plan?" He did his best to sound upbeat, smiling and giving his voice a positive inflection.

Skylar and Anita nodded and slowly stood. Together, the three of them went to Richard's pack. Ethan opened the main compartment and began taking out the contents. Canteen, cook stove, lantern, a windbreaker... His eyes opened in surprise as he took out a flask of Scotch whiskey. He set these items aside, but Skylar cracked the flask and took a swig. She passed it to Anita, who surprised them by also downing a shot.

"You're up, Ethan." Anita held the flask out to him, but he had both hands deep in Richard's pack.

"Hold on, something's stuck in here..." He fiddled around some more until he was able to remove the object that was hanging up. A rolled-up plastic bag wrapped around an oblong object, rubber-banded to hold it in place.

"Here: you drink, I'll open that." Anita traded Ethan the flask for the package. The photographer knocked back a shot, screwing up his facial features in an expression of unpleasantness. "Here's to you, Richard."

By the time he had put the cap back on the bottle, Anita had unfurled the plastic bag from the item, revealing red and white cloth wrapped around something else. Anita unrolled the cloth and held up a flag, red with a white cross in the upper left corner.

"Tongan flag!" Skylar said.

Ethan nodded. "Same exact flag—size and material—as the one he said he found over there. But I saw him planting it in the ground himself."

Anita squinted while looking at the flags. "So he brought a bunch of Tongan flags with him? Why?" She unrolled the rest of them—four all told, plus the one he tried to plant.

"Somebody got to him." Ethan eyed the collapsible poles the flags had been wrapped around, again, the same as the one he had tried to use. "I have no idea why, but he's been bought and paid for to make it look like the Tongans claimed this island first."

While Ethan stuffed the flags into his own pack so as not to leave a false Tongan presence, Skylar pulled Richard's backpack toward her and began rummaging through the rest of its contents. She unzipped a compartment inside the main pack. She wrapped her fingers around smooth steel, looked down and tensed when she recognized what she was looking at.

Skylar glanced up at her two teammates. Both of them still conversed with each other about the ramifications of the flags and who it was that Richard could have been working for...*The Tongans?...the U.N.?...the CIA?!...*

The geologist slipped the gun from Richard's backpack—it was some kind of pistol, but she didn't know anything beyond that—and dropped it without showing it to the others into her own pack. She casually closed the top flap and was turning back around to go back into Richard's pack when Ethan suddenly grabbed it and pulled it toward him.

"Let's see if we can find anything else that would tip him off to being some sort of spy."

"Or mole," Anita added. "Maybe he was bought off by the Tongans. Could be they gave him some cash to plant those flags and to look the other way if evidence was found that proved they weren't the first to land here."

Ethan's hands froze on the pack, and he looked up at Anita. "But the sole survivor we found so far, from the landing party, was confirmed to be a Tongan by our translator." He closed his eyes for a moment as he mentally relived Kai's gruesome dinosaur death, before adding, "Why would Tonga pay him to plant flags when they were actually here?"

Ethan held her gaze for a moment longer, a moment during which Skylar never took her eyes from his, and then he shook his head and delved once again into Richard's bag.

"Maybe something in here will provide more clues..." He pulled out a few more odds and ends from the pack—nothing incriminating or even interesting at all—toiletries, extra batteries, a fire starting kit...

"Ah, wait a minute, what have we here..." He dug deeper into the pack, inside yet another zippered compartment, beneath a foil emergency blanket. He said nothing further as he removed the object from the bag with a smile and held it in his palm for the two women to see.

"Well, well, well, it seems Richard—God rest his soul—saw fit to bring his own mode of outside communication."

Skylar and Anita stared wide-eyed at the Iridium 9555 satellite phone in Ethan's hand. At first, their expressions reflected mild anger at having been misled by Richard. Skylar put a voice to what they were all thinking. "If he had a phone all along, why didn't he use it before, especially with his injuries?"

"No reception down there in the tunnels." Ethan flipped the device over in his hand, looking for the power button. "He watched Lara trying to get a signal and figured, if she can't, then he probably can't either, so why risk it?" He thought about it for a moment and then added, "Or maybe he was planning to get a call out while he was planting his flag back there when I walked in on him."

Anita stared at the phone in Ethan's hand. "Or….maybe he did get a call out. How would we know?"

Ethan lit the phone up and waited for the boot-up screen to indicate it was searching for satellites. "How about if we figure out what Richard was up to later and just see if we can get a call out now?"

"Good idea," Anita said.

"I second that." Skylar cinched up her pack as though ready to hitch a ride out of here right this second.

But it didn't take long for an expression of anger to build on Ethan's face.

"What's the matter?" Anita leaned in over the phone, and Ethan angled the screen so that she and Skylar could see it.

"It's passworded."

"Try taking the battery out and putting it back in," Skylar suggested. "Maybe the password will reset if it loses power?"

Ethan shrugged and carried out that suggestion, but when he powered the device back on, the pesky password prompt was still there. "Now what?"

"Maybe try a couple typical passwords." This from Anita. "His name? 'Password1'? '1234'. That kind of stuff?"

Once again, Ethan followed through with the suggestions, also adding 'explorer' and 'Gaia' to the list, but nothing worked. "I think we've spent enough time on this for now." Ethan dropped the phone into his pack. "We'll take this back with us so we can figure out what he was doing with it. Neither of the two expedition sat-phones were passworded, but he sneaks a phone along he didn't mention to anyone and it's passworded?"

Skylar nodded. "It's got to have to do with the Tongan flag business, whatever that is."

The troubled trio gathered their belongings and donned their backpacks. With a last look around at the scene of so much devastation, they set off up the mountain while smoke belched from the top of the volcano.

CHAPTER 24
United States Embassy, London, England

The CIA case officer known to Richard Eavesley as Baxter picked up the encrypted satellite phone from his desk. He turned it over in his hands, as if considering whether he should use it. He hadn't heard from his mole on the Gaia expedition for an uncomfortable period of time—not since he'd called in shortly after arrival, when they'd found the Tongan survivor. He still didn't even know if that man had been saved.

While aware that too much communication with his man in the field placed him at risk for discovery (he wasn't supposed to have his own sat-phone, first of all, and his expedition teammates would wonder who he was talking to and what about), at the same time, he had that sixth sense about things now. If pressed to explain it, he wouldn't be able to put it into words very well, but it was sort of an ESP that those who spent a lot of time in tradecraft developed. *It was time to make contact.*

Baxter keyed the phone and put it to his hear. He heard a series of clicks and then a ring tone indicating that Eavesley's device was being notified of the call. *Come on, you old mountain man, pick up...*

Baxter wanted to be able to assure his higher-ups in The Company—the ones in charge of the political goals for the Neptune's Inferno project—that a Tongan presence on the island had been established beyond a shadow of a doubt. That was Baxter's sole responsibility, to make sure the Tongans established ownership of the new isle, because if some other country got it, then all bets were off for an American military base in the region.

The news he'd received from Eavesley's first—and so far, only—call had seemed promising indeed, and if pressed by his superiors, he would certainly let them know what he had learned. But if he was to go to them and declare success before the expedition returned, well then he needed a little more information first so as not to make a fool of himself later.

The Tongan, for one thing. Was he alive? Because if he had died, and no other survivors from that first landing party—the one he'd pressured field agent Esau into cajoling the Tongan King to sponsor—had been discovered, then the implements he'd given Richard were paramount. And he had no way of knowing for certain they'd been deployed yet. Would Eavesley get the chance to use them? Would he even try to use them, if given the chance?

Baxter disconnected the call and redialed in order to give Eavesley a second chance to answer. The guy was in the field, after all, with the phone probably jammed down somewhere in his backpack. Give him a chance to get to it...

He lapsed back into his situational thoughts, darker musings. *You don't think Eavesley chickened out, do you?* It was a very serious transgression to simply not uphold one's end of the bargain after entering into an agreement with the CIA, yet it had been known to happen on occasion. People got scared, thought they'd be able to talk their way out of it or just ignore it altogether, as if it would go away. Somehow, though, Eavesley didn't strike him as that type. Back in that pompous club in London, he'd hardly batted an eye before accepting the proposition. *Makes no difference to me who gets that damn rock*, he'd said.

The call went to a generic voicemail, and Baxter decided to leave a message. "As soon as you get this, return the call. Update required."

CHAPTER 25

Skylar took the lead on the hike up. The going was extremely difficult as well as treacherous, the group having to scale mini-mountains of lava while skirting steep drop-offs. Ethan kept watch for boats out across the ocean whenever he could do so without compromising his hiking abilities, but he saw only blue water dotted with whitecaps.

They reached a section where once again, a spire of twisted lava rock necessitated an agile climb out over the edge of the perilous track they followed. To fall off would mean certain death, likely being flayed alive while coming into contact with razor sharp lava rock over and over until falling into the sea below. But even allowing for an overabundance of caution, Ethan could see that something was still not quite right with Skylar.

She took a long time to make her way over a relatively simple obstacle, Ethan noticed. It was as though she was vastly over-weighted, but she wore only her same backpack and carried no additional gear. Yet as he watched, she was constantly having to compensate for being pulled backwards by her heavy pack. Sure, they had taken on some additional equipment scavenged from packs of the fallen, but he and Anita had shared in that burden and they were nowhere near as encumbered. He thought that perhaps Skylar had become injured and didn't want to make it known for fear of being perceived as a burden to the group.

He caught up to her after she almost toppled backwards hopping over a small rise. "Skylar, you look a little shaky. Are you okay? Any injuries?"

The geologist stopped walking and adjusted her pack without looking back while she spoke. "I'm fine, Ethan, thanks for asking."

"The reason I ask is because you keep having to compensate for being pulled backwards." He moved closer to her and went to put a hand on her backpack. "Maybe if you let me adjust your pack, we can—"

"Hands *off*, Ethan! I said I'm fine."

But as she stepped off a low-lying rock, her foot slipped a little and again her pack took her straight down, landing her in a heap on the path.

"Skylar, why don't you let us help you?" Anita caught up to them and stood with her hands on her hips, looking down on the fallen scientist. Skylar pushed herself up to unsteady feet, avoiding eye contact with the others.

Ethan moved until he could see her face. "What is it you're carrying in that pack that makes it so heavy, anyway?"

"It's just my normal gear, including the rock hammers and stuff, a few rock samples from the island to test back in the lab, plus the new gear we took on from Richard's and Joystna's packs."

"Please—you didn't have the shovel when we needed it back there with the allosaurus to dig Anita out. What happened to it?"

"Actually, it turns out that I do have it, I just couldn't find it in the heat of the moment and there was no time to go through the trouble of digging it out from under all my other stuff."

"Let me see it now, then, since you still have it."

There it was, out in the open. A demand, a veiled ultimatum, really. If she didn't let him see, he and Anita could either overpower her and take the pack, or simply leave her behind to fend for herself until she was either killed by one of the prehistoric beasts, ran out of supplies and perished, or got lucky and was able to be at the right place at the right time when the rescue helicopter called by Ethan showed up.

"Shut up, Ethan." She whirled around to face him now. "And you know what? I'm tired of you taking my picture all the time." She pointed to the camera hanging around his neck. "I know you're taking pictures of my ass, you perv."

"Okay, that's enough!" Anita waved an arm in the air, as if to banish all activity. "Ethan, if she says she can make it, then let her make it." Then she turned to Skylar. "But you shouldn't be lead. Let Ethan go first."

Skylar stared Ethan down for a moment before acknowledging Anita's suggestion. "Fine. In fact, you can both go ahead of me." She stepped aside, pressing herself against the wall of the volcano while Ethan and Anita resumed the path upward, hiking past her.

The angle of incline increased as they neared the summit, but Ethan remarked how he considered it a piece of good luck that this avenue, sketchy as it was, afforded them the chance to get close to the summit at all. "Get close to" was the operative phrase, though, since before long, they reached another imposing rock wall. The good news was that it led directly to the summit, the bad that it would require a time consuming, technical climb as before, making use of pitons, ropes and belay systems.

Ethan shrugged off his pack, as did Anita. Skylar removed hers as well, but sat on it, Ethan supposed as a way to make sure no one tried to access it. The team took a break, snacking on power bars and drinking water while they mentally prepared themselves for the task ahead.

"One more climb." Ethan stared up at the fifty-foot wall. "Just one more climb and we'll be at the summit, and I know there's some decent walkable ground up there, as well as a helo-landing zone. We can do this!"

"Your pep-talks suck, Ethan." Skylar stepped into her climbing harness.

"Whatever. The sooner we get up there, the sooner we can find out if that sat-phone is still up there."

"And if it still works," Anita added, immediately regretting the comment.

"You two give any thought as to what we'll have to do if we can't make a rescue call?" Skylar fastened a carabiner to her harness and threaded a rope through it.

Ethan stared up at the summit while he answered. His voice was flat. "We'd have no choice but to camp out until the originally planned pickup time. Setup a base camp on the summit and wait it out for...almost four more days."

A chill came over Anita as she considered the ramifications. "Four more *days*."

Ethan capped his water bottle and started prepping his climbing gear. "Let's hope it doesn't come to that. First things first. We've got a little climb to do."

#

Ethan hammered in what he hoped would be his last piton before making the summit. The climb had gone smoothly, easier than the one on which they had lost Lara. Solid hand- and foot-holds were plentiful and the rock face not quite vertical, meaning he could lean in to the wall for a rest. He even scanned the water far below for boats. Still didn't see any, but the act of doing something to improve their fate, however small, was uplifting, and soon he was on his way up the final few feet to the top.

Ethan hooted as he reached over the lip of the cliff and threw a leg over. He pulled himself up onto the summit. From here, he could look down a gradual, walkable slope and see the devastated area where he had fallen through earlier, some distance below.

"It's nice up here!" he called down to Skylar and Anita. The sailor was already rigged to a climbing harness and testing her first set of holds.

"Hey, Anita, it's easy, but it's not that easy. Give me a minute to set up the belay so I can catch you if you fall, okay?"

"No problem. Actually, why not take my pack up first?" She clipped her backpack to the line and Ethan hauled it up.

"I can haul yours up, too, Skylar. Clip it to the line."

"I want it until I have to climb."

Anita and Ethan exchanged knowing glances, but he didn't push the issue.

"Ready when you are, Anita. Belay on."

"Climber ready. Climbing! " Anita began to climb in earnest, scaling the wall even faster than Ethan had. She paused on a large foothold, a mini-ledge, really, halfway up for a breather.

That's when they all heard the scratching sound. Scrabbling, scraping. Not very loud, but persistent and getting noisier.

"You hear that? What is that?" Skylar stood up from her pack, which she'd been using as a chair.

Neither of her team members responded, so intent were they both on listening to the oncoming noise. Ethan spoke next.

"I've heard that before. It sounds like—" Before he could complete his sentence, Skylar screamed. She pointed to the trail from which they had made their way up the volcano to the bottom of the cliff.

A herd of small chicken-sized creatures flooded up the volcano.

"The ones from inside the cave, right after the earthquake!" Ethan finished his earlier sentence. They all knew they were small but vicious, and apparently meat-eaters. There had to be at least a thousand of them, roughly estimated by eyeballing the seething mass. They ran up onto the climbers' staging area with serious speed. Skylar hefted her pack but tripped as she stumbled the rest of the way to the cliff base.

"Ethan, take my pack!" She clipped it off to a dangling belay rope.

"Oh, now you don't mind, eh? Funny how that works…"

"Ethan, not now!"

"I got it, move!"

"I don't have a rope!"

"What? Where's yours? I thought you rigged it already!"

She glanced up at her pack, now being hauled up the rock face. "I thought it was in there, but—"

"Just go! You can do it without a rope." Ethan eyed the animal pack that had to be only a few seconds away from Skylar now.

Skylar looked back and saw the mob of avian dinosaurs flocking toward her, cackling, screeching, scratching their way across the lava rock. God, how she detested them and their animalistic single-mindedness. She leaped onto the wall in a move Ethan had to give her credit for. She reached the second level of foot and handholds in a perfectly executed jump. And it was a good thing, since the horde of pack-hunters swarmed beneath her only seconds after she left the ground.

Anita looked down to check on the progress of the lizards and saw both Skylar free-climbing up the wall as well as the pack fanning out beneath her, seeming to rise up the face as easily as water poured into a glass.

CHAPTER 26

Skylar pushed up to the next handhold, six inches above her fingertips. She dug her fingers in and leaned into the wall, holding on, knowing that to fall was to be consumed alive. Above her, Anita, who had the benefit of being harnessed and roped in, made a lateral move for a relatively wide ledge about six feet out to her left. She could have opted to go straight up by a more difficult reach, but she did not want to fall and so took the detour, after which would be an easy ascent to the summit.

Ethan leaned over the edge from above, urging on his fellow expedition members while trying not to spook them with the stress in his voice as he watched the mass of predators scramble up the rock toward them.

"Don't look down, just keep climbing, you'll be fine."

But Skylar was not fine. She reached a tricky section of the wall where not being roped in was paralyzing her into inaction. "Anita, help!"

Anita looked down from her own precarious position, almost but not quite to the ledge she sought. "What?"

"I need a rope. Can you drop me one?"

"There's a piton right next to you? Can't you clip one on?"

Skylar shook her head while watching the advancing dino-lizards clatter their way up the face, ever closer to her. "I don't have any, didn't get a chance to get it out of my pack."

Anita frowned and looked down at her waist belt, to which she had clipped extra ropes, carabiners, and a small pick-axe. "I'll see what I can do. But if you can move, you should. Don't wait for me." She took one hand off the wall to reach down to her belt. While she was in the act of unclipping a coil of rope, one of the chicken-things fell from the top of the cliff onto Anita's head.

She beat it away with the hand she had been using to get Skylar's rope, her other hand still holding her to the cliff face, but the motion set her off balance and she teetered backwards. A shocked cry of surprise escaped her lips as she fell. Clipped in to a safety line about ten feet below her, she still faced a twenty-foot fall, upside-down and backwards. The back of her un-helmeted head struck the wall hard, level with Skylar but a few feet to the right.

The horde of avian dinosaurs was almost to both women now, but Skylar had decided on a calculated move and made a jump up to the hold she hadn't wanted to try for unassisted. She made it, clutching the jagged sliver of rock like life itself, digging her toes into the rock face and leaning in.

This left Anita alone and still exposed at the level of the dinosaurs. She was groggy from the head concussion and slow to begin pulling herself up. But Ethan's voice, yelling at the top of his lungs, brought her around.

"Pull up, Anita. Move! You've got to pull up, now!"

Anita strained her abdominal muscles to reach up for the safety line that had kept her from falling all the way to the base of the cliff. The fingers of her right hand had just clutched around the rope when the first of the reptiles got to her. She let go of her newly won rope, falling back to the rock upside-down again as the bird-like beasts rolled over her body. She swept the first few away, dropping them to the ground below where they skittered around, stunned but unharmed. Unrelenting masses soon replaced their missing ranks, however, and Anita was ravaged beyond help by the pint-sized predators.

She fought as long as she could, flashing on a sailing experience where a friend had died after being tangled in a rope and dragged overboard. After that, Anita had always carried a small, folding knife to cut lines. She pulled it from her waistband now and opened it one-handed with a motion she had practiced many times long ago. She hacked at a few of the primordial attackers with it before it was ripped away as if in a strong wind.

She screamed until her face was eaten off by tiny, razor sharp teeth while she dangled there, one of her eyeballs rolling down the cliff before being fought over by dueling dinosaurs. Her pitiful cries soon succumbed to the ravenous animals, choked off by the lizards' ripping apart her mouth, consuming the features of her face.

Ethan forced himself to look away and shifted his attention from Anita to Skylar.

The geologist was still on the move, and the bulk of the predatory horde now stayed with Anita's corpse, decomposing the flesh as if in a time-lapse photography movie of the sea eroding an island over the millennia. Skylar reached for another handhold, gripping it at the same instant as a lone individual latched onto her ankle. She pulled her leg back and dashed the creature's tiny head into the rock face, caving it in until it sloughed off and fell into the seething crowd below, ingested along with Anita's rapidly disappearing innards.

"Grab this, Skylar." Ethan called down from the edge, not so far above, now. He dropped a length of rope down to her. It landed right next to her, but still she clung to the wall.

"Don't look down. You've got some time, they're below you now. Focus on the climb." They both knew he meant, *You've got some time, they're eating Anita now.*

Skylar took a deep breath and gripped the rope with one hand, testing it. When she saw that it held fast, she planted both feet flat against the wall and transferred her other hand to the rope as well.

Below her, a snapping sound echoed off the wall as the chicken-monsters bit through Anita's safety rope. Then came a sickening thud as the mutilated corpse thudded onto the ground at the base of the cliff, bones cracking. Skylar blocked it out and pulled herself up by the rope. When she reached the edge, Ethan grabbed her by an arm and hauled her up and over.

"Good. You made it. Here's your pack." He handed her the backpack. She eyeballed the fasteners, checking to see if they were still closed. It made Ethan mad that she was so selfish as to be concerned about her personal belongings, whatever they were, when Anita had just been so horribly killed before their eyes. But he was in no mood to argue about it now, and even more… He didn't like to admit it, but he'd rather have Skylar with him than no one to face whatever remaining Hell awaited him on this isle.

"I never opened it. We've got to trust each other now, Skylar. It's just you and me."

CHAPTER 27

The rain fell almost as soon as they made it onto the summit. It fell straight down, not driven by wind, and at least it was warm, tropical precipitation not likely to last long without the presence of a storm. Still, it reminded Ethan they were alone and exposed to the elements, with no hope of rescue anytime soon unless they could find that sat-phone.

He glanced at Skylar, who sat on the ground with her legs out in front of her, back resting against her pack, still breathing hard from the exhausting climb. "We should get going. Before…"

"I know." She rose and put on her backpack, struggling to lift it long enough to slip an arm through the strap. Ethan eyed her suspiciously but said nothing. Right now, he didn't care what was in that pack. Out of an expedition of eight, only two were still alive, and he was one of them. He intended to keep it that way, everything else be damned.

Skylar managed to get her pack on and they walked off toward the area where the original Slope Team had fallen through to the lake. It felt to Ethan, looking at it now, like that had been days or even weeks ago, even though it was only yesterday. The ground was spongy in spots, and mini-geysers of lava bubbled up in others.

"Over here." Ethan pointed and picked up his pace as he recognized the swath of destruction from which he had barely escaped the first time he was here. "Keep your distance from the edge, it may not be stable ground around it."

They skirted the edge of the collapsed ground, moving toward a rocky section traversed with deep cracks but which had not completely fallen away. "The crack the phone fell into is somewhere over here." Ethan continued to lead the way, moving ahead of Skylar. Volcanic vapors mixed with the falling rain to reduce visibility. As they neared the target area, scratching sounds came from somewhere out of sight in the fog.

Skylar's head swiveled instantly toward the disquieting noise. "Hear that? Oh God, they're coming!" She sounded not quite like she was on the verge of tears, but the closest he'd heard her come to that, and it worried him. She'd always seemed so level-headed. The last thing he needed was for her to come undone now.

Ethan stopped moving and turned around. "Calm down, Skylar. We're almost there. Stay focused and keep moving."

She remained still for a few seconds more, head on a swivel as she searched for the source of the scrabbling. "It's those little ones that killed Anita, I just know it. They followed us up here, Ethan!"

"We don't know that, and even if it is, don't do anything to provoke them. Be quiet!"

"Okay! Shut up before they hear us!"

Ethan narrowed his eyes at her for just a second before turning around and continuing toward the cluster of crevices where he last saw the phone. Skylar resumed walking as well. The scratching sound died away for a bit but then resumed, a little louder, though there was still nothing to see.

Up ahead, Ethan waved an arm in an energetic gesture, beckoning Skylar to hurry up and get to him. When she reached him, he was kneeling next to a crevice and pointing into it.

"Look," he whispered, pointing down and to the left, where a glimmer of silver contrasted with the brownish rock.

"Is that it?" Skylar wiped the rain from her eyes as she gazed into the volcanic rip.

Ethan nodded. "It at least looks like it's in one piece, too." He studied the crack some more before shaking his head. "Not sure if I can get down in there, though. Awfully tight fit…"

Indeed, the crack was barely wide enough to allow a human to fit. Ethan was not overweight, but anybody would have a hard time slipping into the jagged rip, which extended for some ways below where the phone lay.

"I can fit." Skylar shrugged out of her pack, then glanced up at Ethan as she set it down, aware she would have to leave it unattended while she went after the phone. Ethan, not wanting her to change her mind for this reason, whatever it was she was hiding in the pack, quickly looked away toward the perimeter, where the scratching sounds drew nearer.

"I'll keep watch. You just get that phone."

Skylar switched on her headlamp and descended into the hole. The crevice was narrow enough that she could place one hand and one leg on either side of it and ease herself down. She had to go slow, but she made steady progress toward the phone. At least down here, she was sheltered from the rain and couldn't hear the incessant grating noise of the chicken-dinos running around.

The opening jogged left as she neared the phone, and that's when Skylar glimpsed a view that took her breath away. Far below the rip, she could see the water of the lake. This crevice went all the way through the volcano's slope, and then there was about fifty feet to the lake. Luckily, the phone had landed on an indentation of rock a few feet before it would have dropped all the way to the lake.

Skylar inched her body lower until she was within grasping range of the sat-phone. She wedged herself into position with her legs and then reached out and took the device.

#

Ethan saw the first dinosaur about five minutes after he left Skylar in the crevice. As he skirted the perimeter of the summit zone around the tapestry of cracks and crevices where the phone lay, one of the small avian reptiles hopped up onto an outcropping of lava rock and perched there. It cocked its head to one side and then emitted a series of clicks and chirps.

Ethan picked up a small piece of rock and side-armed it at what he thought of as a scout, though he had no idea if that was true. The simple creature scuttled out of the way and ran into the mist. A minute later, about a hundred of them appeared in its place. *You were a scout, you little bastard!* Not even close to as many as the mob that took down Anita, but a formidable presence nonetheless. Ethan threw a rock behind and to the right of them, hoping to send them off in that direction.

The tactic worked for a few of them, but most of the herd animals continued on their way toward the human. Ethan glanced over at Skylar but he didn't see her; she hadn't yet emerged from the hole. Right about now, he wished he was down there, too. He'd be safer there, from the looks of things. The pack of diminutive predators flocked back together after being interrupted by the rock. They turned toward him.

Ethan wasn't sure if he could fight off this many of the creatures. Half as many, he thought he could deal with. But as it was…he was worried. All it would take was one misstep, a single slip-up, and… Images of Anita's gruesome demise played inside his skull.

He steeled himself to fight, even going so far as to slip a small fixed blade hunting knife from its sheath, but he had no idea what he planned to actually do with it. He recalled how Anita had tried in vain to use a knife… The first sensations of panic were welling up inside him when the group of herd animals suddenly shifted direction, away from him. They trotted further down the volcanic slope, out of sight into the misty fog. Ethan breathed a sigh of relief, but knew he shouldn't push his good luck windfall. The predators could return at any moment. He was about to call over to Skylar to see how she was doing when he felt the ground shake under his feet.

Ethan turned toward where he sensed the trembling originate. A small spire of rock toppled over. He began to worry they were having an aftershock from the earthquake, when a towering form emerged from lower down on the slope.

At first, the photographer mistook it for a collapsing section of mountain, so large was the shape. But as it continued its way up the outer slope, the figure registered in Ethan's mind as something else entirely.

The elongated structure he had thought of as a dislodged boulder was attached to something else. As it rose higher up the slope, Ethan could see that he was looking not at any kind of geological process, but rather a *head*… A massive, gargantuan head attached to a body large enough to be proportional. Two tiny arms dangled from the front. Dull yellow structures interlaced inside the head. A black orb. All of these things registered fleetingly in Ethan's mind before the two words that he knew identified what it was he was looking at materialized: *Tyrannosaurus rex.*

Seeing it also reconfirmed his earlier assumption that it was an allosaurus that had almost killed Anita down in the cavern. This beast was significantly larger, the forearms much shorter. Ethan Jones forced himself to face the nightmarish reality that he was staring at a living, breathing *T. rex.*

How can this be? He didn't know why it should be more unbelievable for a *T. rex* to be roaming around this godforsaken rock than all of the other dinosaurs he'd encountered so far, but for some reason it was. And yet it was real as could be, climbing up the slope, all those millions of years' worth of evolutionary instinct driving it right toward him. He dropped his knife and started to run. No kind of weapon he carried was going to defend him from this mega-beast. He would just have to lighten his load as much as possible and get away from it.

And when he could....snap some pictures. But not now. Now it was time to run.

#

Skylar clawed her way back to the top of the crevice, the sat-phone tucked safely in her pants pocket while she climbed. When she reached the opening, she didn't climb all the way out right away, but instead looked around like a prairie dog with its head out of its burrow. Where were those horrible chicken dinosaurs? Where was Ethan?

Not seeing either, she climbed the rest of the way out of the hole up onto the relatively flat ground of the summit. Then she sat on a rock and pulled out the phone, turning it over in her hands, appraising its condition. It certainly looked beat up, with more than a few scrapes and scratches, but the screen was not cracked and the battery compartment was sealed. It didn't appear to have gotten wet.

Moment of truth... She held down the device's power button, holding her breath, praying silently it would do something. For a couple of long seconds, nothing happened, and she felt her heart sink to her stomach. Then the screen lit up. The word *Yes!* escaped her lips in a hiss as she watched the phone boot up. *Now to wait for a signal...*

She made sure the phone had an unobstructed view of the sky and then looked around the summit while she waited for it to lock onto its satellites. Still no sign of either Ethan or the dinosaurs. She figured he was probably off taking pictures in his never-ending quest for a cover shot on National Geographic or whatever. Good for him. She just wanted to get off this hellish rock in one piece with her bag of diamonds. Then she'd retire in peace, no more schlepping around the globe, living out of campsites for months at a time. She'd paid her dues. These gems were her severance package, damn it.

The phone beeped, alerting her that it had acquired a signal and was ready to make and receive calls. Skylar opened the contacts and quickly activated the number for their U.N. handlers. She glanced around the summit again while listening to the phone ring on the other end. Still no activity. As she expected, the call went to a voicemail; being in the South Pacific, she knew New York was seventeen hours ahead, which would put it late at night there. The tone sounded, indicating the recording was on. She spoke into the phone in a hushed voice, looking around to make sure Ethan was not within earshot.

She talked rapidly, afraid the connection would somehow be lost due to some quirk of atmospherics or a technical glitch.

"This Skylar Hanson from the United Nations Gaia Expedition to the newly formed island of *Hunga Tonga- Ha'apai*, in the South Pacific. The expedition has met with disaster. This island is very unstable, still subject to massive amounts of volcanic activity and earthquakes, but even worse than that...it's somehow full of...full of monsters—dinosaurs, I think. I know it sounds crazy, but I am of sound mind and am the only surviving member of the expedition."

She took one deep breath before continuing. "Here is the official recommendation of the expedition: In order to avert a major world disaster should these dangerous creatures escape, as well as to eliminate an extremely hazardous physical environment while removing all possibility of warring over new land, proceed as follows... Deliver the 'code red' aerial bomb to destabilize the island and send it back into the sea—it's far too dangerous to risk these monsters escaping, and the entire island is a geologically unstable biohazard. If upon arrival you don't hear from me or see me atop the summit, blow it to Hell. Unlikely I will survive that long, anyway. Good luck all. Dr. Skylar Hanson, over and out."

CHAPTER 28

Skylar disconnected the call and smiled to herself. She had set everything in motion. She would get through this on her own. She—

"Skylar!"

The geologist whipped her head around to see Ethan standing behind her, hands on his hips, an angry scowl on his face. "What the hell is going on? I just heard you mention dropping a bomb on the island, and that I wasn't alive. Care to explain yourself?"

Skylar produced the gun she had taken from Richard's backpack and leveled the barrel at Ethan's chest.

"Because you're not alive, Ethan."

Skylar's finger pulled back on the trigger but just then the earth shook, knocking her slightly off balance as the gun fired. The bullet went wide left, grazing Ethan's right arm, which dripped blood onto the scorched rock.

The ground continued to shake, knocking both of them off balance. By the time they regained their feet, the unbelievably large head of the *T. rex* was visible behind where Ethan had been standing. Skylar fired off two rounds at it, both of them disappearing somewhere into the monster's chin. The reptile paused for one second before resuming its course toward the humans.

Making matters worse, the source of the skittering, scratching noises made itself known as a herd of the chicken-sized beasts that materialized from behind them. Skylar spun and blasted off three more rounds while Ethan ran off to the right without a word. Fortunately for Skylar, the *T. rex* chased after Ethan, who thought that might happen but wasn't sure how many bullets Skylar had left and so opted for what he perceived as the lesser of two evils.

He found earlier that by bobbing and weaving his way down the slope, taking cover for a few seconds at a time among different rock formations, that he could trick the giant dinosaur into thinking he had run another way. He wasn't sure about the animal's sense of smell, how good it was, but figured that the sulfurous gasses wafting through the air might be preventing it from detecting him. At least he hoped so.

Skylar fired off more rounds into the herd of birdlike attackers. Surprisingly, they scattered into multiple directions, leaving those that remained ineffectual against her raging boots. She stamped on a few of the lingering chicken-like beasts, until those that remained scuttled out of sight down the volcanic slope.

She looked around for Ethan and the *T. rex*, but they were both somewhere out of sight. She hoped the terrible lizard would consume Ethan, and with him, her witness to attempted murder, but unless she saw him dead, she wasn't going to believe it. He had managed to survive out there with it while she was in the crevice, after all. Besides, she still needed to worry about herself. These small predators could return at any moment.

Skylar checked her weapon's clip: only a single shot remaining. She should have searched Richard's backpack more carefully to see if he had brought along extra ammunition. Frowning, she moved off in search of Ethan. She had reported him as dead! Even though, should they both end up testifying before some committee back in New York, it was only his word against hers as to what happened here, her voicemail saying she was the only survivor would be the final nail in her coffin... Unless she could manage to hunt Ethan down. Hunt him down and kill him the same way these God-awful dinosaurs were doing to the rest of the expedition members. Then she would simply dump his bullet-riddled body into a lava pit and say he was carried off by a *T. Rex*. She made a mental note to recover his cameras after she killed him in order to have proof of the animal threat here.

One shot left, though, will have to be very careful... She now wished she hadn't ditched her pick axe in order to collect more diamonds. It would come in handy as a backup weapon in case the first shot didn't take Ethan down. Not to mention against the animals. But after she dispatched Ethan, she would scavenge his equipment.

The geologist moved off cautiously onto the summit, listening carefully as she picked her way across the uneven slope. She was under no illusions that it would be a simple matter to locate her quarry. The summit was full of nooks and crannies, caves and crevices in which he could hide. And she wasn't his only threat, either. That tyrannosaur gave him extra incentive to hunker down somewhere, and fast. But that could be a good thing, since it meant he was less likely to try to get to another part of the island altogether. He would almost certainly hide out somewhere nearby.

It also occurred to her, as she slinked around a jagged outcropping of rock, that she wasn't exactly immune from danger herself simply because she had a gun with one bullet. Ethan was like a cornered animal now, and everyone knew cornered animals could be extremely dangerous. He could leap out from behind a rock at any moment—

She heard a noise up ahead and froze. Something like a rock being dislodged. "Come on out, Ethan. Let's talk about this. If you come at me, you leave me no choice."

Seconds passed in silence. "Ethan! Don't do anything stupid. If—"

But it wasn't Ethan who crept out from behind the rock. It was a strange dinosaur, sort of like a modern day monitor lizard but much larger, and with a large sail fin on its back. A narrow, forked tongue flicked in and out of its mouth as it moved slowly toward Skylar.

Shit. She didn't see how at first the outcropping could conceal such sizable bulk, but as the lizard moved out of the way, she realized it had crawled up and out of a hole in the ground. While she was staring at this, the animal lunged at her. Skylar had no choice but to use her final bullet. She fired at the animal's chest and hit it in the neck. A fount of blood geysered out of its throat and the big lizard stopped in its tracks, lowering its head.

Skylar didn't stick around to see if the damage she had done would have a lasting effect. She ran off to her right, down the slope, skidding here and there on loose rock but not stopping for anything until she was out of sight of the beast. She lay on her backside and listened for telltale signs of the animal's approach, hearing none. Apparently, she had dealt it enough damage that it had decided she wasn't worth the effort. That was her final bullet, though.

She looked at the gun still clutched in her right hand. It was now useless, except as a means to scare Ethan, since he had no way to know it was empty. But that didn't give her a lot of comfort. Even if he was fooled by the impotent firearm, she now had no easy way to kill him. She would have to trick him into thinking she had ammo left, tie him up, and then…do something messy.

She wasn't looking forward to it, but she didn't see what choice she had at this point. Keeping the gun out on the ground in front of her, in case Ethan showed up, she decided enough time had passed that it was worth checking if she had received any kind of acknowledging message on the sat-phone in reply to her voicemail. It would be good to know when that helicopter was going to get here. She lifted her butt off the ground and removed the device from her back pocket.

Her heart sank before she even looked at the screen. She could feel a web of cracked glass. *You idiot, you sat on the phone!* She flashed on her battle with the sail-fin lizard and realized with an uncomfortable start what must have happened. When she had backed away from the beast down the slope and fell, she had landed hard on her backside—and the phone. She cursed herself for putting the fragile device in her back pocket instead of a front one, or even better, stowing it away in her pack again.

What was she thinking? Now she would have no way to coordinate her pickup when the helicopter or plane or whatever it was they were sending arrived to drop the bomb. Sure, she had told them in the voicemail to proceed with the bombing if they didn't hear from her, but that was just showmanship to make herself appear more altruistic—that she was willing to sacrifice herself for the greater good. She had planned all along to call them when she heard the engine and have them pick her up before they dropped the bomb. Surely the U.N. would supply them with a sat-phone that had the expedition's number in it? She supposed she may be able to contact the plane using her handheld radio, but in reality, she suspected she was going to have to make herself physically visible by standing out on the summit waving some kind of signal flag.

And that meant making herself vulnerable to the dinosaurs. And Ethan.

She stared at the empty gun in front of her and strategized.

#

Ethan Jones actually managed a grin as he stared with one eye through his camera's viewfinder. The *T. rex's* eyeball filled the lens, but from a safe enough distance. He was hunkered down in a cave so small as to be claustrophobic, but right now, he wouldn't have it any other way. If he could barely fit, it meant that nothing else big enough to eat him would be able to, either. And that was more than fine with him.

He snapped off a few more shots of the incredible creature and then dropped the camera around his neck. Besides the fact that a rogue *T. rex* roamed about within throwing distance, and that one of his expedition members—the only surviving one—had gone crazy and tried to kill him, something worried him. When he had picked his way down the slope on the way to finding this cave, he had seen more cysts hatching. Quite a few more. He didn't stick around to see what was going to emerge from them, but for all he knew, there could be a dozen *T. rex*es about to come looking for human prey.

The sharp *crack* of another cyst hatching open somewhere in the immediate vicinity of his hideout interrupted his grim thoughts. He thought about what was happening on this island, about how it was that these dinosaurs had come to be here. He knew the entire island had formed when an undersea volcano had spewed up magma from deep inside the Earth out of the ocean floor. Was it possible that these…cysts…these strange rocks, were carried up by the magma, and able to withstand the heat without shattering or dissolving? That in so doing they had transported through the eons a set of animals that should be extinct? How many of them could there be? Hundreds, he knew that for sure. Thousands? How many more waited to be ejected from the depths of the Earth and hatched into the present?

He ruminated over these unsettling thoughts while the popping of more cysts continued all around him outside. How long would the island itself even hold together? *Crack...* At this rate, the whole fiery rock would be in pieces before that bomb Skylar phoned in even got here...

And speaking of Skylar... Ethan began to look through his pack. He would have to do something about her if he was going to get off of this island alive.

CHAPTER 29

Nuku'alofa, Tonga

CIA Special Agent Valea Esau summoned all the restraint he could muster in order to politely thank King Nau's guard and assistant before he was ushered into the Malo Nau's suite. He had to keep up the illusion that everything was all right, just another day in paradise. He knew that Nau's people knew him only as a local mechanic who worked on the royal fleet, but at the same time, the sheer number of personal visits to the king's palace would seem out of place for a man of his stature. Valea knew the rumor mill would start to swirl if this kept up, but he was pretty sure this would be the last visit for a long time.

The door to the suite was closed as soon as he stepped inside and a smiling Nau greeted him ebulliently before moving to the bar. But this time, Nau waved him over.

"Please, Malo, no drinks today. Time is very short and what I have to say is entirely sobering."

Nau halted a few steps from the row of crystal decanters and frowned, but then took a seat opposite Valea without having made a drink. "Tell me, Valea, what is happening?"

"The U.N. received a call from Expedition Gaia—the single surviving member of it."

The king's bushy eyebrows made a tent above his eyes. "All except for one are…"

"Seven out of eight are dead. A rescue mission is being prepared as we speak to pick up the sole survivor, a geologist, Skylar Hanson. I wanted you to know, because…"

"Because they are going to bomb the island?"

Valea nodded wordlessly.

"Was no evidence of my landing party discovered?"

The g-man made uneasy eye contact with the king before going on. "Actually, Malo, they did." He related what he knew, which was relayed to him from his U.K. agent, Baxter. "Our asset on the trip—now deceased—got out a satellite call stating that they had found a Tongan man alive but in very bad shape. Those were all the details I had at that time, and Hanson's call made no further mention of it."

The king looked confused. "I do not understand, Valea. As unfortunate as that it is for my people on the landing party, discovering one of them means that they did in fact land on the island, which is good for our political situation as it relates to the Neptune's Inferno project, is it not?"

"Yes, and I even had our mole plant some Tongan flags to bolster the presence."

The king reared his head back. "Then what on Earth is the problem?"

Valea took a deep breath while he tried to think of how he was going to explain the dinosaurs. "Maybe it is time for those drinks after all, Your Majesty."

The king smiled and made the trip to his bar, then returned with two glasses of amber liquid. Then he listened as Valea recounted Skylar's report of living dinosaurs rampaging across the island, infesting it.

"I do not want these monsters invading Tonga. Perhaps it would be better to bomb the island, after all." The king held up a finger before continuing. "Assuming, of course, that Tonga receives its fee, as you promised."

"Of course, Your Majesty."

CHAPTER 30

How long would it take for the aircraft to arrive? Skylar wasn't sure, but she did know one thing: she needed to be atop the summit when it showed up. Not to be visible to that aircraft was tantamount to suicide. At the same time, she couldn't simply hang around in plain sight on the summit unless she wanted to ring a dinner bell for the cornucopia of prehistoric super-predators that roamed this fiery isle.

Ethan could come for her, too. She couldn't rule it out. She'd tried to shoot him, so he may take an offensive approach for Round 2. So where to position herself up here so that she could wait around in as least jeopardy as possible? She didn't think the air support would take more than twenty-four hours at the most to arrive, and possibly as few as eight. She needed to get ready.

Skylar looked about from her current position. Wedged in between a cluster of rocks that formed sort of a teepee over her head, she was nice and safe from a predatory perspective, but it wouldn't do for when that aircraft arrived. Reluctantly, she emerged from the natural shelter and glanced about the summit slope. She had worked her way down slope and now would have to regain some ground to make the summit peak again.

Empty gun in one hand (for Ethan) and a small knife in the other (for everything else), she began making her way up. The rain, falling harder now, made her footing less secure; she had to place each step with care. Despite the fact that her heavy pack slowed her down considerably, she would not consider lightening her load of precious gems. She was not about to go through all of this for anything less than a life-changing financial windfall. She spidered her way up the slope, ducking into rock formations for cover here and there, emerging again after listening for animals.

When she had nearly reached the summit, a large head peeked over a rocky ledge. A tongue flicked in and out of a mouth. A humongous lizard, perhaps the size of a Guinness Book of World Records alligator, stared at her with black eyes. Then she heard skittering off to her right, turned and saw more of the chicken-things coming her way.

This was simply not going to work. Eyeing the summit, her best hope was to hang out inside the crevice where she'd found the sat-phone, then wait and pop out when she heard the aircraft. But there was no way she was going to reach that with these dinosaurs blocking the way. What's more, it wasn't exactly a comfortable, safe spot where she could lay down and rest. She'd have to hang on vertically, wedged in there until the plane or helicopter got here. If she fell asleep or tired and lost her grip, she'd fall all the way through to the lake.

Operating on the principle that there had to be something better than that—hoping there was, anyway—Skylar altered her upward course in favor of one that took her laterally around the summit rather than higher. For some reason, there were more dinosaurs up top. That didn't mean she didn't have to fight a few off here and there, though. The little ones. Fortunately, she didn't encounter a large mob of them like on the cliff, but instead, smaller gangs of 10-20 roamed the hillside, seemingly at random. When they neared her, she stomped on one with her boots and the others would scatter and get back into formation some distance away.

She trudged on, now with a rip in her pant leg where a smear of blood showed through. *Need. This. To. End.* But wishing wouldn't make it so, and she forced herself to march onward. To where, she wasn't sure, but somewhere, anywhere, to hide from the dinosaurs and that would also afford her at least a chance of spotting the aircraft before it dropped the bomb.

After a while, she began to cough, too. She'd never been a smoker, was not asthmatic, and so she knew it must be the poor air quality here on the island. But it hadn't been this bad when she'd first got here. Looking up toward the summit, she saw clouds of ash darkening the sky, raining slowly down upon her as they mixed with the actual rain to form sludgy, gray pustules of ash that stuck to her skin.

She zoned into a kind of hiking trance, daydreaming of better times gone by while devoting a part of her brain to a kind of auto-pilot, remaining alert for the sights and sounds of dinosaurs and the volcano itself. She still had a lot of time to pass, and, as she glanced down again at her bleeding leg while hearing a screech from an unknown animal somewhere above on the slope, she knew she would not last out in the open until the aircraft arrived. When she had made it about three-quarters of the way around the volcano, though, she still hadn't seen a good opportunity for a hiding place.

Skylar trudged on, trying to silence her inner pessimist, the one that kept shouting, *If six out of eight people on your expedition are dead, what makes you think you're going to get out of this alive, huh? What makes you so special, besides that backpack full of diamonds?*

The wind shifted direction, a downdraft, and she went off on another coughing jag. This one forced her to stop walking, to hunch over and dry heave for a minute. When she looked up again, she spotted a plastic object on the slope, a few yards down from her. Black, pretty small, looked like it would fit in a hand. She moved off down the slope to check it out. Reaching it, she could see what it was without picking it up. A canteen screw cap.

By itself, it was no big deal. Trash, sure. But it wasn't like she was going to add even an ounce of weight to her load to clean up this hell-hole. It wasn't her cap, that was the important thing.

It was Ethan's. She pictured his pack, the water bottle clipped to the outside. No doubt when he'd gone running down the slope after she'd shot at him, or possibly evading that *T. rex*, it had come off then, or he'd not had enough time to screw the cap back on. She looked up from the cap to stare down the slope. This is where he'd gone. And he hadn't come back, so if Ethan had found somewhere safe down there, maybe she could, too. Problem was, the higher up the slope she was, the easier it would be to gain the attention of the aircraft.

But when a herd of the chicken-dinos came tumbling down the hill, looking like an avalanche of feathers and claws, screeching and clucking, Skylar knew she didn't have a choice. Down the slope she went, the same way Ethan had gone. Her feet slid out from under her a couple of times, and she shredded the skin on her palms pushing off jagged rocks to keep herself moving, but she made progress down the mountain.

Skylar craned her neck to look back up the mountain. The herd still rolled down after her. This one was large, too, still not as large as the one on the cliff, but she would not be able to boot-stomp her way through them should they overtake her. Dismayed at having put her body through so much trauma without widening the gap between her and the predatory threat, she continued ever lower. She sought the nearest shelter that offered the faintest hope of survival in the face of this aggregate killer. A jumble of boulders looked like it might do, but as she ducked down to scoot between them, one of them start to wobble. Figuring something was about to hatch, Skylar backed out, glanced up at the group of avian dinosaurs (closer now), and ran downhill.

It seemed like she trod down forever, but in reality, only a few minutes went by before she came to a flat but narrow tract of land about a third of the way down from the summit. Quickly, she took her bearings while resting with her hands on her knees, breathing heavily. The sound of the herd clattered across the slope from above, relentless in their pursuit. To her right, the track continued around the cinder cone, while to the left it ran for some distance before being interrupted by a confused jumble of rocks.

She took off left, hoping the rocks strewn about would block the progress of the horde. When she reached them, she had to find a route over the first boulders. She eyed them carefully to see if they might be yet-to-hatch cysts, but they didn't move at all and didn't have the somewhat rounded characteristic she'd noticed on those that had produced dinosaurs.

Skylar climbed halfway up one of the rocks before the weight of her diamond-laden pack pulled her back to the ground with a thud. She scrambled to her feet and glanced back at the oncoming dinosaurs. If this barrier was hard for her to get across, she hoped it would be for them, too. She hefted her pack and chucked it over the rock. Then she tried scaling the obstacle again, this time reaching the top and dropping down in between the jumble of rocks.

She had expected to climb over all the rocks and continue on with the track, but looking to her left, she was surprised to see the opening to a medium-sized cave. High enough to walk into without stooping and wide enough to drive a car through, she knew this was as good as it was going to get for the time being.

Skylar flipped on her headlamp and moved into the cave. She would have liked to survey it for a bit before entering, but with the herd nipping at her heels, she wanted to remove herself from their line of sight—and probably smell—as soon as humanly possible. She ran inside, the beam of her light sweeping the walls as she turned left and right. A pillar of rounded stone running from floor to ceiling looked like a good thing to put between her and the dinosaurs, should they make their way in here. She went to it and shrugged off her pack.

As soon as it hit the ground, she felt a strong hand grip her arm and wrench it back. Her gun went flying, and she heard it clatter into the cave wall. Then she felt the grip leave her arm and the pounding of footsteps across the cave floor, followed by the voice of Ethan Jones.

"Hands up, Skylar. It seems you've found my little hideaway. I'd offer you a cup of tea, but… I'm supposed to be dead for one thing, remember?"

"Let me explain."

"You can start by opening that precious pack of yours."

"Why are you so concerned about my pack?" She glared at him across the cave, eyes fixed on the gun. She still had a glimmer in her eye that made Ethan uncomfortable. It was a gleam of sorts that wasn't usually found on someone with a gun trained on them.

"I'm concerned, Skylar, because you're so worried about it that you would lie, cheat and steal for it. So let's have a look." He waved the gun at her pack.

With obvious reluctance, Skylar eased down to her knees, grimacing in pain, and brought her fingers to the clasp on her backpack.

"Just unclip it and step away, over there." He waved the gun at a clear area about ten feet away. He figured she wouldn't try to run away without her pack, knowing that survivability on this island with no gear of any kind was not something the odds makers in Vegas would favor very highly.

Skylar unclasped her pack and moved slowly away from it.

CHAPTER 31

Ethan flipped off his headlamp and set it on the ground pointing up, so that it illuminated the cave but wasn't blinding Skylar. He did this without altering his aim with the gun, which was still pointing at Skylar's heart. "Use one hand to take your headlamp off and toss it on the ground. No funny business."

Skylar did as she was told, and when the beam was no longer blinding Ethan, he could see the strands of her sweaty, dark hair caked onto soot-laden skin, framing the sly grin on her face. "Attagirl. Now, you stay right there and we won't have a problem."

Ethan walked over, keeping the gun aimed at Skylar, and grabbed her backpack. He picked it up and dumped the contents onto the ground in a heap. There were only a few camping or expeditionary type items inside. The rest was a pile of raw diamonds, including two very large chunks, gleaming dully under the weak artificial light in the cave. Ethan's jaw dropped as he stared at the pile of concentrated wealth.

"Are those… Diamonds?" he gasped.

"I don't know," Skylar shrugged. "They superficially look like diamonds, but there's no way for me to say for sure without taking them back to the lab for testing. That's why I'm collecting them."

Ethan laughed at this. "Right, because you need fifty pounds or so of them for lab testing." He took a step closer to her with the gun. "You know damn well that these are some kind of valuable precious gems, probably diamonds, that's why you've gone through so much trouble to lug them around."

"They appear to be gemstones, Ethan, but as I said, I need to get them to a lab to be sure."

Ethan cackled derisively. "Yes, and I'm sure that as soon as you determine they're diamonds in a lab, you'll just rush right out and turn them all over to the U.N., yes?" He stared at her with contempt. "So that's what you've been up to! A plan for your own personal gain? You're a geologist, for Christ's sake." He waved an arm at the walls of the cave, where thick veins of diamond ore criss-crossed the walls. "You killed people for these stupid rocks? They're just rocks, look at them! People died because you couldn't carry your own weight, had to borrow other people's gear because you ditched yours so that you could carry these damned rocks!"

In a near rage, he picked up one of the diamonds and hurled it at Skylar. It was a serious throw, baseball-pitcher style, his body spinning around so that he faced away from her after he unloaded his pitch. She reached down and withdrew a fixed blade knife from her boot.

"Now get out of my cave." Ethan turned back around and jerked the gun toward the exit. He saw the knife in her hand and laughed derisively. Skylar's gaze moved to the light at the entrance, then back to Ethan. She slowly shook her head.

"I don't think so." She waved the knife at him.

"Bring a knife to a gunfight, did you? I knew you weren't that smart…" He nodded at her pack and the spilled diamonds. "…but I didn't think you were that dumb."

"I won't be going anywhere. The little ones are out there. Just leave me alone, and I'll do the same to you."

"I'm the one with the gun, Skylar."

"The gun with no bullets."

Ethan checked the chamber of the weapon, his eyes widening when he realized it was in fact empty. Enraged, he dropped the gun and moved to the diamond heap. He picked up the largest stone, the football-sized chunk, and tossed it into a pool of bubbling lava in a corner of the cave. Then he bent down to pick up another…

Skylar shrieked, "Stop it! What about this: I'll split them with you. Fifty-fifty—you take half of what's left."

Ethan cocked his head to one side, as if thinking intently. "Oh really? Now that's funny, because just a few seconds ago you said they weren't diamonds, that you didn't know if they were valuable."

"That's right, Ethan, I don't know, that's why I want them lab tested. But as you pointed out, they certainly look valuable, don't they? So whatever they are, I'm proposing to split them with you, half and half."

Ethan snorted. "And then what?"

Skylar shrugged. "We can cooperate in a civil manner to get off this island alive, and from there…" She smiled at him. "We go our separate ways."

Ethan stared at her for a long moment as though considering the offer, but then he shook his head as if disgusted. "No, Skylar. I have no interest in them. I only want you to face consequences for what you've done here. And these diamonds, they belong here, to this volcano, not to you, you greedy bitch…"

He bent down to scoop of a handful of diamonds to throw them into the lava. Skylar charged at him with the knife. Just as she reached him, the ground shook violently, sections of the cave walls shearing off and crumbling around them.

Both of them froze for a moment, staring at each other to make sure the other wouldn't make the first move as the ground continued to shake. A deep rumbling issued from the rear, darkened portion of the cave. Ethan's eyes widened in fear as he watched a gigantic cyst boulder roll its way toward the mouth of the cave—right toward him and Skylar. The round rock left no room on either side of it as it spun down the cave's main chamber.

He turned and ran for the exit. Skylar spun around and saw the rock coming, but paused to scrounge up her backpack, hastily shoving what little gear she still had along with some of the diamonds into it before the rock got close enough that she abandoned the remaining heap of gemstones. She ran for the exit after Ethan, the boulder jarring along behind her.

Outside the cave, Ethan saw the high sides of jumbled boulders and knew he wouldn't have time to climb them before the rolling rock reached him. He was pretty sure Skylar wasn't going to make it, having stopped to grab her pack. But that was her problem. That rock was going to steamroll right over her and then mow him down, too, unless he could think of something fast. He ran all the way to the edge of the path, where a sheer drop-off fell away for about a hundred feet to the wave-splashed base of the volcano.

He glanced back at the cave, where Skylar now burst out of the entrance, pack dangling from one shoulder, the massive stone looming immediately behind her. He had zero time to set up a climbing rig. Fear pumping through his veins, he ditched his pack, tossing it out to the side, and then turned so that his back faced the edge of the cliff. He backed down over it, hands clutching the rim. Maybe the thing would just roll right over him as it plummeted over the edge. Or maybe it would shatter the bones in his hands, causing him to lose his grip…

A guttural yell from Skylar tore him from his thoughts as she sprinted toward the edge, face a mask of sheer terror.

Ethan glimpsed a solid handhold—a micro-ledge—about a foot beneath the edge, and brought first one hand, then the other to it. He moved his feet about, searching for a toe hold, but contacted only smooth rock face. He would just have to hold on with his fingers for dear life. He could feel the ground trembling above him as the boulder came nearer. He would only have to hang on for a few more seconds.

Skylar's face said it all as she trammeled to the edge—pure, mindless panic—she was one stumble, one muscle cramp—away from certain death. The boulder (or was it a massive cyst containing some fully grown brontosaurus or God knows what kind of extinct behemoth?)—Ethan couldn't be sure, it was moving so fast—took a stray bounce as it rolled over a rock outcropping. The massive rock bounced high, on an even plane with Skylar's head, and she launched her body into a dive— headlong toward the edge of the cliff.

The wayward boulder flew over Skylar's body as she dove over the precipice. The gigantic rock plunged down the slope of the volcano, impacting at the bottom with a crash they could hear all the way up here. But Ethan wasn't watching the rock. He watched Skylar. The geologist looked like she was about to follow the rock on the same trajectory, but at the last moment, she hooked one of her feet on the edge of the cliff, keeping her dangling on the face upside down.

The woman had some agility, for after only a couple of seconds, she began to right herself by seeking new hand- and foot-holds. Ethan was comfortable enough where he was for the time being, but he wasn't about to risk his life for this person who had tried to kill him. He wouldn't hasten her demise, either, nor would he help her at any cost to his own chances for survival.

He called over to her as she stabilized somewhat, body in a very awkward position, almost sideways on that rock face, about four feet below the edge. "Drop your pack! It's weighing you down!"

Skylar's backpack dangled precariously from one shoulder, placing undue strain on that arm. She had to keep moving her hand to keep purchase on the vapor-thin hold she had.

"All you have to do is let it slide off, Skylar."

But Skylar didn't pursue that option. Whether out of greed or a genuine fear that ditching the pack would somehow cause her to lose her grip, Ethan didn't know. But she stubbornly held onto that pack as she shifted her weight on the cliff. She started to cry, clinging to that rock wall, sobbing gently, trying not to move.

But Ethan couldn't hang there and watch somebody die. Even though she had tried to take his own life. The thought of doing nothing while she fell to her death was not something he wanted to live with. "Hold on, I'll get up and get a rope to you."

Ethan climbed back up over the edge of the cliff. Slowly, deliberately. He wasn't about to make a mistake for her. When he had both arms firmly over the edge, he threw himself up and over and ran to his pack. He unclipped the coil of rope from the outside and returned to the edge. He knew there was no time for a proper rig. He would just have to try to manhandle her up, manually pull her hand over hand once he got her the rope. He was pretty sure he could do it. If not, he'd have to let go, but at least it gave her a chance. The way she was situated on that cliff, she didn't have much time left.

"Skylar, here comes the rope. You're going to have to grab it. Wrap it around you if you can. Whatever you do, hold on good. Then I'll pull you up. Ready?"

"Hurry, please."

Ethan stood there, perched on the edge of the cliff, eyeballing the best place to drop the rope. He didn't want it to land on her and actually cause her to fall. But from the shaky sound of her voice and the precarious hold she had on the wall, he knew he had to act now. He fed the rope down to her rather than dropping the unfurled coil, not wanting to dislodge her.

To his horror, she turned her head and looked at him, eyes wide, and fell a split second before the end of the rope reached her.

She did not scream, but simply plummeted down the wall. Her body smashed on a lava rock precipice about halfway down before continuing to be flayed along the outside of the volcano, effectively skinned alive on the way down until coming to a dead rest on a lava shelf by the sea, backpack bursting like a diamond shrapnel bomb.

CHAPTER 32

Ethan knelt at the top of the cliff, hanging his head. Skylar was gone. As much as he detested her actions, he disliked the fact that he was now alone on this island even more. Ethan Jones, the last survivor. Would he be able to hold onto that title? He got up and went over to his pack, put it on and took stock of his surroundings.

He looked up, first, anything to avert his attention from Skylar's destroyed body below. But the brownish haze of drifting soot wasn't all that comforting, either. The volcano on which he stood continued to belch fire and ash. At ground level, he heard the clamoring of claws on rock somewhere off to his right, on the other side of the jumble of scorched rock piles they had climbed over to reach the cave by the ledge.

It sounded to him like a single large individual and not a herd of small ones. Whatever was coming from his right, he would make his way to the left. He walked to the rocky border to his left and was preparing to scale it, to continue on this track around the island, when he heard a new noise.

Not the scratching of claws or any sound produced by animals. This was wholly artificial, blessedly human-made. Ethan stepped off the rocks he'd been preparing to climb and walked out to the edge of the cliff. *Don't look down at Skylar. Don't think about her.*

The sound was muffled and coming from far off. He scanned the waters for a ship, but saw only the monotonous blue of uninterrupted ocean. Then it hit him with a start: aircraft! He craned his neck to look up to the sky, but the haze spewed by the volcano reduced visibility considerably, and he could see nothing.

Gradually, the sound became more distinct, and Ethan was pretty sure it came from a helicopter. It sounded like it had at first been behind him, on the other side of the volcano, and was now coming around the island to his left. Then it hit him all at once— the significance of an aircraft. He flashed on Skylar's sat-phone call— *I know it sounds crazy, but I am the only surviving member of the expedition*—and then her recommending they drop a bomb.

The aircraft is here!

A jolt of adrenaline coursed through his body. The presence of air support was at the same time extremely positive and negative. On the one hand, it meant the opportunity for rescue. The only practical opportunity, really, since the last remaining satellite phone had plummeted with Skylar to her death and was no doubt shattered into pieces. He mentally kicked himself for not taking it from her when he had the chance, in the cave. On the other, darker hand—that aircraft—per Skylar's instructions which they thought represented the team as a whole, was here to drop a bomb to destroy this island and send it back into the depths of the sea. If he was on it when that happened…

He had to find a way to get the attention of the—

The thrum of motors grew suddenly louder as the aircraft rounded the island. Ethan spotted it—a large, unmarked military-style chopper, definitely not the same commercial Bell that had brought them here—as it skirted the island a few hundred feet above the summit. He watched as the 'copter passed by him above, continuing around the island. They were making a scout pass, he knew, checking it out upon arrival, probably looking for Skylar and any other survivors. He had to get their attention somehow before they proceeded with dropping the bomb.

Ethan threw open his pack and considered his options. In a couple of minutes, the helicopter would be back around to his side of the island, and he wanted to be ready to try something to make contact with them. He tossed items around in his pack, looking for anything that might offer some utility in this situation. No sat-phone, but he had a walkie talkie. He grabbed that and turned it on. Aircraft didn't usually monitor walkie talkie channels, but maybe in this case they were? They should be, but then again they were probably expecting to be in contact via sat-phone.

He flipped through the channels, looking for a broadcast, but as expected, there was no noise, not even static, on any of them. Maybe they weren't transmitting, but listening? So he started with channel 9, the one designated for emergencies in most parts of the world.

"Mayday, mayday, mayday... Ethan Jones here, from United Nations Expedition Gaia. Do you read, over?" He repeated this a couple of times and then, after receiving no reply, scrolled through the channels. He broadcast the same message one time on each frequency, then scanned through the channels again.

At the end of the second time around, he still had heard nothing. Ethan dropped the radio in frustration, mentally beating himself up. Stupid walkie talkie idea. Aviators didn't use those. He'd wasted his precious time. By now, the helo had passed him by and was making another pass around the island. Quickly, he rummaged through his pack again, tossing items out, searching for anything that—there!

He saw his own reflection for a moment and recognized his old signal mirror. Sort of a Boy Scout item that reminded him more of his childhood nature walks than something he would ever actually need to depend on, Ethan realized now that this was exactly what he needed.

The din of the helo motor became louder as the craft circled around to Ethan's side of the island again. He readied the mirror, practicing angling it to catch the sunlight and reflect it back up to where he though the chopper would be. But when the aircraft flew into his line of sight, it was much lower than it had been on the previous passes and he had to adjust his aim with the mirror. By the time he got it right, a dense patch of volcanic smog had belched from the volcano and drifted between Ethan and the helicopter, obscuring the flash from his mirror.

The rescue vehicle continued again around the island, and Ethan hung his head in defeat. They had not seen him. What was he going to do? He looked up at the summit, where if anything, the smoke that discharged from the vent became even thicker. Pretty soon, they might not be able to see the island at all. He considered whether he should try to make his way back to the top of the summit for a better chance at being seen. But as it was, he couldn't even see the summit anymore, so choked was it in belched fog. Not only that, but as he looked up the slope, he could *see* a pack of the small chicken dinosaurs lurking on the steep slope. They were probably being forced down due to poor air quality as well. Maybe he should go down slope instead?

He was studying the portions of the slope below him when he heard the helicopter come around once again. It was even lower this time, making the engines very loud even though the craft itself was obscured in a smoky haze. And then he heard it—a male voice issued through a megaphone.

"ATTENTION: Skylar Hanson. We are trying to make contact with you. Respond to sat-phone call or else contact us via UHF radio channel 22..." The message repeated as the helo flew slowly around the volcano.

Ethan ran to his pack and scrambled to pull out the radio again. *I tried the radio already. Now you're ready, okay... Now where'd I put that thing...*

While Ethan shuffled the items around inside his pack looking for the radio, he heard a commotion behind him. He ignored it, concentrating instead on finding that walkie-talkie. That single item was his ticket out of here. He got a glimpse of black plastic and gripped it. There!

But just as he yanked the radio from the bag, he felt an impact on the back of his neck, sharp claws digging into his skin and a beak or a tooth or something sharp pecking at the top of his head. He screamed as chunks of his hair and scalp were ripped from his head. Hectic warbling sounds came from the dinosaurs as they clucked and cooed while attacking.

Ethan brought his right fist up to knock off the individual on his head, but in his haste forgot that he was still holding the radio with that hand. The small dinosaur retaliated by gripping two of Ethan's fingers in its short beak and whipping its head back and forth in a tearing motion. Ethan flailed his arm to knock it away, and the creature sailed over the cliff...

Along with the radio.

Now there were two broken radios at the bottom of that cliff—his and Skylar's. Ethan tried to recall where the packs of his dead expedition members were around the island; unlike the sat-phones, every team member had carried a walkie talkie. Maybe he could get to one of them in time? But then his finger started throbbing, the pain intense. He looked at it and saw white bone sticking through the flesh.

Suddenly, more dinosaur bodies fell on him, scratching and pecking. He didn't know how many, but it was clear the pack he'd seen up on the cliff had reached him. Through the fog of his panicky self-defense, throwing dinosaurs off his peck-riddled body, he heard the thrum of rotors approaching yet again. *How many chances do you think you're going to have, Ethan? Any time around now could be their last before they decide, enough already, drop the bomb...*

Ethan yelled as he whirled around, attempting to generate sufficient centrifugal force to throw his attackers off. A couple of them did go flying, but a few stubbornly remained, scratching and tearing at his flesh with feral abandon.

Then came the megaphone voice again: "Dr. Hanson: we have orders to destroy this entire island with bombs. We will search the island for survivors for the next fifteen minutes. After that, we'll be low on fuel and will be forced to drop the bombs and return to base. Repeat..."

Ethan stared out at the helo as it flew out of sight again around the island. Fifteen minutes! Even if he couldn't contact them, he had to get off the island—swim out into the ocean if nothing else. To stay on this land was suicidal.

He peered over the cliff to see if he could reach the ocean that way. No way could he free-climb it, and much of his climbing gear had been left behind on the other walls they'd scaled and had to leave in a hurry. He thought he might be able to rig something out of what he had if he had considerably more time, like a half an hour, but fifteen minutes? No way. That wasn't sufficient time to both set the gear up and then make the descent, leaving enough minutes left over to swim away from the exploding isle...

It wasn't possible to jump far enough out to do a cliff-dive style entry into the ocean, either. He'd hit the rocky tide pool area where Skylar had impacted.

Meanwhile, the dinosaur problem was getting worse here. A large sail-fin lizard poked its head over the rocks to his right, and a squadron of four pterodactyls appeared in the sky off to his left, heading his way. Even if he could rig a climbing system in time, those flying predators would pick him right off the wall.

Ethan turned and looked back into the cave where he'd confronted Skylar. He remembered the huge boulder rolling out of it. It had come from somewhere. It was time to see where. He had nowhere else to go.

The photographer shouldered his pack and ran back inside the cave.

CHAPTER 33

Ethan flipped on his flashlight once he entered the outer cave. He ran past the area where he made Skylar drop her backpack, saw the little pile of scattered diamonds there that she'd left behind in a hurry, and kept going toward the rear of the cave. He hadn't gone this far back earlier, as he had only sought a hiding place from the crazy Skylar after she'd tried to shoot him. Now it was time to see if it led anywhere.

He saw fresh gouges of rock like a track where the rolling stone had passed. He reached what looked like the end of the cave, but was surprised to see an empty space in the floor. Leaning over and shining his light beam down into it, he could see a vertical drop of perhaps ten feet, then a passage continuing down at a walkable slope. The walls in front of him bore heavy chinks where the big boulder had sat. He supposed the earthquake and its aftershocks had dislodged it, causing it to roll down slope and out of the cave.

Ethan hung by his hands from the edge of the opening and let himself drop the rest of the way. He landed on bended knees, the ground solid lava rock as was the main cave. He was grateful for that, as one of his biggest fears about this island was that he could jump onto what looked like solid rock only to find out the hard way that it was molten lava covered with a layer of black soot.

The walls here glittered with thick diamond veins snaking their way in and out of the passage walls. Ethan adjusted his rucksack straps and began following this new passage down into the bowels of the glittering jewelcano.

He wished he still had his headlamp so that he could have both hands free instead of having to use one to hold a flashlight, but it had been torn off during the cliff struggle with the boulder. So when he tripped and fell headlong, hands splayed out in front of him as he hit the ground, it was with great dismay when he heard a cracking sound followed by his light blinking out.

"Damn!" he called out to no one. He felt around for the broken light, found it, tried the switch just in case it still worked but no luck. He was pretty sure he had a backup light somewhere in his pack, but he wasn't sure exactly where and now he'd have to dig through everything looking for it in the pitch black darkness. He took off his pack and started to do just that—although he was all too aware of the time limit imposed by the bomb drop, he had no desire to trip and fall headlong into a pool of bubbling lava—when he heard a soft rasping sound somewhere ahead in the void.

Something was there. Ethan rummaged through his pack faster, wishing he'd taken time to organize things a little better. Then his fingers passed over a zipper compartment and he opened it up. *Please tell me I put an extra light in here...* He felt around inside the pouch—a Swiss Army knife, extra batteries, a pen...aha! A small flashlight. He pressed the button and was relieved to see his pack flood with white light.

But when he took the light out of the pack shined it ahead of him to illuminate the source of the noise, he was not relieved to see a giant snake coiled in the passageway not ten feet away from him.

Ethan had seen plenty of snakes in the wild, from huge boa constrictors in the Amazon rain forest to twenty-foot long pythons in the Florida Everglades, but he'd never seen anything like this. This snake had to have a girth of at least three feet, with the head a weighty, triangular structure that looked as if it would have no trouble swallowing a human whole. The only thing Ethan saw to his advantage was that so far, at least, it moved slowly. Right now, in fact, it wasn't making forward progress at all, the sudden presence of light perhaps causing it to stop in its tracks. It lay there in a tight coil, head raised above its body, the black tongue flicking rapidly in and out, no doubt tracking his chemical scent.

Ethan quietly removed a hunting knife from his pack before putting his things back inside and putting it back on. During this activity, the snake stretched its head out closer to him but did not actually move its body. Ethan wielded the blade in his right hand with the light in his left. He slowly rose to his feet, eyeing the path ahead. He hoped he would be able to squeak by to one side of the monstrous animal, but its skin touched both sides of the cave walls. Not that he looked forward to battling the creature, but most of all, he really didn't have time for this. He and the snake would both be blown to bits in about...he consulted his watch...twelve minutes if he couldn't get past this thing *and* find a way out of here.

Ethan was not the pessimistic type, but even he had to admit to himself that his situation did not look good. He didn't know what kind of bomb they had, but that helicopter was huge, and this island was unstable enough as it was. He had to get past this snake, without engaging it, and now. He considered making a dash for it on the left side, high-jumping over the coils and running away. But he knew that sudden movement would spur the reptile into fight mode, and that snakes were very fast strikers.

Think, Ethan, think! He played his light beam around the walls and noticed they were pocked with holes—a result of bubbles in the lava as it rapidly cooled and solidified. They made such good hand- and foot-holds that the walls here were almost like the artificial rock climbing walls he'd occasionally trained on at home. No ropes needed. He sure wished he had that headlamp, though, but he'd just have to hold the flashlight between his teeth.

He stepped up to the left-side wall and began to climb. He first gave himself the necessary vertical clearance to pass over the snake, then began traversing the wall off to his right, over the serpentine threat. He looked down on its tight coils as he passed. What was it even doing here? Were snakes around during dinosaur times? He supposed so. These thoughts served to distract him as he moved, keeping him calm and less prone to panic. Before he knew it, he was ten feet past the snake. He began descending while continuing to move laterally, and when he hit the ground again, he was twenty feet from the serpent, which had still not moved.

Ethan breathed a sigh of relief while he shone his beam ahead. The passageway continued, but at a steeper downward slope. He moved out at a jog, his mind now sounding a new alarm: *What if this path doesn't lead anywhere, what if it dead-ends up ahead? You don't have enough time to go all the way back, past the snake again and up to the cliff...*

He silenced the inner voice and kept moving down the passage. The ceiling became lower after a while, forcing him to stoop, slowing his progress a little. He glanced at his watch again: only six minutes left. Where did this path lead? He kept going, dodging low-hanging stalactites here and there. The tunnel became even more laden with diamonds, so much so that the reflections of his light actually blinded him, further slowing his pace.

Just as Ethan began to worry that the passageway might not dead end, but instead would continue on unending until his time ran out, the blinding light of the diamonds stopped. An opening lay ahead. He ran as fast as he possibly could toward it while crouching. He stumbled out onto a platform set into the volcano's inner cliff. It offered a spectacular view of the lake from about twenty-five feet up.

Three problems, though, Ethan thought, glancing yet again at his timepiece. One: With only three minutes left, he was almost certain to be inside the volcano when the bomb detonated. Two: he didn't have time to do a slow climb down, even without ropes. Three: this ledge was crawling with large snakes. There had to be at least fifty like the one he had just passed. It made him nauseous merely to look at the hideous den of them. Even as he stood there, a cyst cracked open to his left, releasing another gigantic mega-python to wriggle out onto the platform. The bomb was the only thing that took his mind off of it.

The bomb! He'd wasted another minute watching the snakes and evaluating his situation. He didn't know what he was going to do. But as he looked down on the lake, he saw the circle of sunlight in the middle, and it triggered an idea that, as feeble as it was, represented all he had.

If he were in the water under the volcano's opening, there wouldn't be as much rock to collapse on him. That was it. That was all he could come up with. But with 120 seconds remaining until detonation, he had to act right now.

Ethan cinched tight the straps on his pack and eyeballed the few patches of open ground through the snakes to the edge.

Then he ran, knowing he only had to streak past about a hundred snakes for all of three seconds before he reached the edge. His legs pumped as hard as they ever had in his life, his blood rushing through his veins, his heart pounding. All around him his peripheral vision registered serpentine movement, his ears the hissing of dozens of snakes.

And then his right boot was pushing off the edge of the ledge and he was flying through the air to the water below.

CHAPTER 34

Ethan hit the lake with a splash and started to kick. His injured finger flared with excruciating pain, but he swam through it. He'd gone a few strokes when he heard—and felt through the water—a massive *boom.*

His time had run out.

He could already hear massive slabs of rock falling from the sides of the volcano's inner slope. He swam as fast as he could for the middle of the lake, but his heavy backpack was pulling him under. He peeled it off and was about to ditch it and continue swimming when he thought about the single heaviest item it contained: a small scuba diving rig. He'd brought it along almost as an afterthought, not at all sure if he'd really need it, but on all of his adventures around the world, his underwater photos had set him apart from his colleagues. They were all on equal footing on a safari jeep, shooting lions chasing zebras with a zoom lens, but when Ethan slipped into a watering hole with a waterproof camera and emerged with unrivaled photos of water buffalo drinking, he knew that from then on, some type of dive gear would always be a part of his kit.

As the volcano began to crumble around him, he freed the mesh dive bag containing a mask, fins, and a small "pony" tank of air with an attached breathing mouthpiece. He let his backpack drift away. It was do or die, now, literally. Do what, he didn't exactly know. His original plan was simply to get to the middle of the lake, out of the direct path of rock falling from above. And he could do that. But the scuba gear opened up other options. He put the stuff on and kicked—much faster now thanks to the fins—to the middle of the lake, moving across a demarcation of dark to light, as if experiencing an eclipse.

Thunderous splashes came from not too far away from him as he swam—chunks of rock falling from high above—but he kept propelling himself forward and soon found himself in the very center of the lake, where the least rock fell.

Ethan spun around in a circle. So this was it. This was where he would die. Looking up, his view of the sky actually widened as more and more rock calved off and disintegrated on its way down to the lake—soon to be no longer a lake but part of the Pacific Ocean once more.

He put his face in the water, mask on, in order to look down. He instantly regretted it. A large mosasaur or maybe plesiosaur (he wasn't sure), like the one that ate George, glided past him. Perhaps forty feet away. Yet it paid him no mind, simply transiting across the lake. It, too, wanted only to escape the destruction.

The photographer lifted his head from the water and glanced up one more time, spinning in a circle. The mountain was crumbling. He glanced back to the ledge from which he'd jumped and saw the multitude of giant super-snakes slithering over the edge into the lake as it crumbled.

Deciding he'd rather die looking for a way out than treading water waiting to be crushed or eaten alive, Ethan clenched the mouthpiece between his teeth and slipped beneath the surface, where the waves had picked up due to the sheer volume of falling rock. He could feel the pressure waves from the explosion rock his body as he descended. He wished he had a dive light. He still had his regular flashlight, but it wasn't made for being submerged and doubted it would last long.

He shone the beam down, wondering how deep the lake was. He couldn't see the bottom and the water was clear. That worried him. It could be two thousand feet deep for he knew, brimming with thought-to-be-extinct sea monsters. It was like swimming over an open abyss, a hadal zone exposed to the surface. He angled toward the side of the lake, seeking the underwater walls. Maybe, just maybe, he could find a tunnel or an opening of some kind that led out to the open sea, now that the overall structure was coming apart.

Strange shapes glided past him in the inky twilight, but he ignored them and kicked even harder for the edge. His light was still holding up, but he thought it might be attracting predators so he switched it off, saving it for if and when he truly needed it. Some daylight still penetrated here.

Ethan listened to the soft, raspy hiss of his breathing through the regulator as he finned his way toward the wall. He could just barely see it now, a dark mass materializing out of the deep blue. It occurred to him as he swam that if a rock did hit him down here, at least its impact would be diminished by the water over his head. All around him he could hear pieces of the volcano dropping into the lake from high above.

He flicked on his flashlight as he neared the wall and was relieved to see that it still worked. He saw glittering in front of him. This threw him off, although still he didn't stop—he could not stop—until he realized that veins of diamond ran through this part of the rock, too. He reached the wall, looked quickly left and right, saw a giant sea monster of some kind a ways off to his left— a long, slender, twisting thing—and he went right.

Ethan's flashlight started to flicker as he aimed the beam along the wall. Its seal was starting to fail. It wasn't pitch black here, but it would be far harder to discern an opening in the wall without the artificial light. He fin-kicked along, a few feet away from the wall as he searched for an underwater exit to the crumbling volcano. The wall was smooth but not regular; it was concave in some sections, straight in others, which made it difficult to look for a break. And then his light winked off and didn't come back on. He hit it a few times with his hand, trying to jar it back to life, but to no avail.

He let the useless hunk of plastic drop into the void and resigned himself to his fate. He was going to die here, alone in the middle of a bombed-out volcano, surrounded by hideous monsters dredged up from the bowels of the Earth and the depths of time. No one would ever even find his body or his cameras, with the proof they contained of the hellish events that transpired here.

Ethan had begun to consider giving up on swimming, to just sit still in one place and wait for the end, reflecting on his life with what little time he had left, when an orange glow caught his eye. Down low, maybe forty feet underneath him. That was kind of deep for him to go with his tiny air tank, since he was already about forty feet down, but he didn't have much else to lose. He might as well die trying to accomplish something, to find a way out.

The photographer angled his head downward and kicked toward the fiery light. As he neared it, he knew what he was seeing: a fresh lava flow, hot magma issuing from the rocks directly into the water. He'd seen it before, in Hawaii, and had taken spectacular video and still shots of it then, so he knew what to expect. He also knew that it meant there was likely an opening being cut through the rock by the liquid fire. He kicked faster down toward it.

Huge booms of massive rock slabs hitting the lake's surface assaulted his ears as he reached the underwater lava flow. Exercising much less caution than he normally would around this kind of volcanic activity, Ethan swam past the billowing magma into what looked like an open space. A tongue of fire licked his calf, and he felt the burn as he kicked reflexively away, deeper into the open pocket. By the time his leg stopped burning, Ethan knew he had entered a chamber, at least. He still didn't know if it led anywhere, but he kicked back toward what looked like the end. He couldn't help but think the entire thing could cave in on him at any moment, but this is the route he'd opted to take.

A glowing tendril of fire lit the submerged cave along the right side. He followed it back and down until his heart leaped. A narrow hole, in the rear wall of the cave, transitioned into a tunnel brimming with running magma.

He stroked with his arms and legs to enter the opening before some freak current—or sea creature—sucked him back out into the maelstrom that was the open lake. The tunnel narrowed but still afforded him with room to swim through, and light to see by courtesy of running magma. He bolted through it as fast as he could, now concerned not only about where it led, but also about his air supply. The little pony bottle he breathed out of was not meant for prolonged scuba diving by itself. It was supposed to be a supplemental bottle, a backup of reserve air or mixed gas supply, not a main tank. And certainly not in overhead environments or deep water, and he currently found himself in both.

With nothing he could do about it, though, Ethan power-stroked ahead through the tunnel, hoping against hope that it would lead out of the volcano. He heard a deep grating noise behind him and snapped his head back in time to see a huge section of tunnel collapse in his wake. He eked even more speed and power from his aching muscles as he power-finned on.

Finally, as cave-ins and collapses grew more frequent, he saw a lightening of the water ahead. Sunlight! Open water! He didn't think the tunnel had doubled back on itself into the lake, and he was looking at the sun-dappled middle portion, but there was only one way to find out.

Ethan swam to the light, the tunnel now lying straight rather than at a downward slope. Yes! So much light, it had to be the open ocean and not the inside of the volcano, even in the center portion. Magma spurted everywhere here, but he didn't care. He swam through it as if he had done it every day since he was born, a firewater human in his natural environment. He only hoped the entire mountain wouldn't collapse in on him before he exited the tunnel.

He reached the opening to the sea, gripped an edge and pulled himself out. Suddenly, another large mosasaur, easily the size of an adult blue whale, swam at him from the left, around a rocky protuberance. His hand snaked to the dive knife strapped to his calf. He grabbed it while he watched the powerful sea-beast slither toward him.

Ethan knew that merely sinking the blade into the mosasaur's flank would do almost nothing, like pinpricking a tiger through its fur. He had to find a sensitive spot if his little knife was to be effective. With a fish, like a shark, the gills were a known soft spot, but this thing—a pliosaur or maybe a mosasaur—didn't have gills; it was a reptile, and as such, had to breathe air. That left somewhere on the head, but he had run out of time to strategize.

The prehistoric animal curled around him in a tight ball, as if coiling to strike, bringing one of its humungous, black eyes past Ethan's face. He lashed out and sunk the blade firmly into the creature's pupil as it made an exploratory pass. He heard a weird grunty squeal from the animal before it turned and fled straight out into the ocean.

Gotcha!

The knife was still embedded in the eye, so Ethan was weaponless now, but he was happy enough to have survived this encounter. *One step at a time...*

And then, as he went to take his next breath, Ethan suddenly found he had no more air to pull.

CHAPTER 35

Ethan tried inhaling again, straining his lungs, but still no air came. He glanced up at the surface and saw the light way up there, perhaps seventy-five feet away.

You can do it!

At least his empty tank was small. A full scuba rig would create a lot more drag in the water, slowing him down. Fatigue had set in, though, from all the high-speed swimming, the battle with the mosasaur and the general stress. He was about to ditch his tank altogether to lighten his load when he remembered something from a scuba class long ago. Even if a tank is empty at depth, as the diver ascends, the air in the tank will expand due to the lessening pressure. If a breath cannot be pulled at seventy-five feet, for example, by the time he reached thirty-three feet, there may be a breath or two to be had from that same tank.

Ethan kicked hard for the surface, keeping his regulator mouthpiece in place. Even though he had no weapon now, he couldn't help but spin around in circles as he ascended, on the lookout for marine predators. He eyed some distant forms at the edge of his visibility, but saw no direct threats. Most of the animals were probably coping with the explosion, he figured, like he was.

He remembered to keep his airway open as he rose, humming through his mouthpiece to ensure his lungs were not closed off, meaning they could suffer an air embolism, bursting with the expanding volume as pressure decreased. *Speaking of which...*he tried to inhale and was rewarded with a small breath of air. Enough to keep him going until the shimmering silver sea surface loomed right above him, just above his outstretched fingertips.

Ethan broke the surface and spit out his regulator. His eyes registered the smoky sky as he gasped in great lungfuls of air, exulting in the oxygen, at being alive, however tenuous that condition may be. He let his empty scuba rig drop into the deep. He tread water while turning in a circle. What was there around him now? Open sea...the island, or what was left of it, anyway, about a hundred feet in front of him. Entire sections of it still buckled and crumbled, the rumbling carrying far out onto the ocean and even farther below it.

He swam farther away from the sinking isle. He had heard that the suction created by sinking ships could pull swimmers down with them, and wondered now if that same principle held true for sinking islands. He knew he might also be swamped by waves created by the sudden influx of mega-tons' worth of material into the ocean. When he felt he was a safe distance away, Ethan tread water and turned in a slow 360-degree arc.

He heard the helicopter before he saw it, the unmistakable drone of a motor over the sea breeze across his ears, the waves rushing past and the rumbling of rock breaking up. When he did finally lay eyes on the machine, Ethan was dismayed to see it flying straight out to sea out from behind the island. At least its altitude was low, but still. As a person in the water visible from above, it was like being able to spot a coconut drifting on the ocean. He needed some way of signaling them, and fast.

He took a quick inventory of his possessions, lamenting now that he'd ditched his pack. All he had on him was a waterproof camera clipped to a belt loop of his shorts, a pair of swim fins, and a mask and snorkel. He needed that walkie talkie now, that was for sure. Or even the signal mirror...

His mask!

He ripped it off his head and looked at its construction. Smooth glass face plate with clear silicone skirt and strap. He cupped it in his two hands and held it up to the sun, tilting it this way and that to see if he could get the glass to catch light...

Yes! A glint of reflected sunlight temporarily blinded him as he got the angle just right. But it had been directed back toward him, not at the helicopter. Now he had to aim it the right way. Ethan turned his body and tried again, this time facing the glass toward the departing aircraft. Beads of water on the mask were causing the reflection to be unpredictable, so he wiped them away and aimed again.

Come on...

The specter of being left here alone, floating in the Pacific Ocean off a destroyed island full of prehistoric monsters, also forced into the water like rats from a sinking ship, was so palpable that he almost dropped the mask. He forced himself to steady his nerves, to maintain his composure, and tilted the mask so that it would catch the sun while facing the aircraft.

Ethan was rewarded with a piercing gleam of light lancing toward the helo. He held the glass steady until the chopper passed in front of it, then shifted the mask slowly and carefully to the left, following the craft with the light beam. Confident he could hold the mask's position with one hand, he raised the other as high into the air as he could and waved.

Here, over here—right here!

And then a large wave, coming from the direction of the now submerged island, rolled over him, ripping the mask from his hands. He dove after it, but the wave tumbled him around and he couldn't find it. Dark, menacing shapes moved about below. He held his breath and swam underwater anyway, looking for the mask until he needed air. He broke the surface, defeated. He was a dead man swimming.

And then he heard the engine change in pitch. He looked up at the helo, far to his left now, and saw it bank into a turn.

\#

Ethan gripped the edge of the rescue basket as soon as it reached the water after being lowered from the helicopter. The solid feel of the basket gave him great comfort. A huge sense of relief flooded through him as he heard the voice of the winch operator above in the aircraft calling down to him: "Climb in, hold on and we'll pull you up!"

Easier said than done, Ethan thought. The sea was choppy to begin with, stirred from above by winds and below by the undersea avalanche of the crumbling mountain. Add to that the rotor wash from the helicopter, and Ethan found himself in a whipped-up soup that threatened to smash his head into the side of the cage and swamp him for good. The chopper descended a couple of more feet, dipping the basket just low enough to allow Ethan to throw a leg over.

He pulled himself into the basket, a cage-like structure with an open top and two orange flotation cushions affixed to either side. "Go!" he shouted up to the winch operator. Slowly, the cage climbed, dripping water as it left the ocean. Ethan allowed himself to relax a bit. He took a deep breath and leaned his head back against the bars. He had made it! He—Wait, what was that?

His head had tilted to the right while resting, so that he was looking down into the water, but it was the movement that caught his attention. A slender dark shape, but very long, longer than the chopper. As it moved, it turned, its color transitioning from dark to light. Ethan realized he was looking at a creature propelling itself quickly and rotating as it swam, doing a barrel roll from back to belly and back again, twisting and rolling as it moved forward.

Ethan wasn't sure what it was. Normally, he would call it a "weird shark" or maybe even a whale, but not here, not on this little island paradise. One word kept surfacing from the depths of his subconscious.

Liopleurodon.

Ethan sat bolt upright in the basket and eyed the monster more carefully. The creature possessed not two, but *four* flippers and a tail that seemed to have no flukes, it just came to an end like an eel. *So strange.* Yet there was nothing strange about what the animal was doing. Ethan had been direct witness to enough acts of predation over the last couple of days to know an animal getting ready to strike when he saw one.

He looked up at the helicopter only to see the winch man with his head turned inward, talking someone inside the aircraft. Ethan bellowed up to him. "Can you go any faster with this thing?"

The equipment operator quickly turned back around and looked down at the basket and Ethan. "We don't like to go too fast because it can set the cable to swinging. Why, is there some—?"

The *Liopleurodon* rushed out of the water at a forty-five-degree angle, toward the rescue basket—toward Ethan. He saw the elongated set of jaws open wide. As if in slow motion, he saw the water streaming from its open maw. It was coming for him, leaping right out of the water straight for its prey.

For a brief moment, Ethan considered hunkering down in the bottom of the cage, but wasn't confident the two-foot high steel bars would provide much protection. This thing looked like it could swallow the whole damned cage, with him in it, right down its slimy gullet. Instead, he sprung upward, hands grasping the cable that was reeling up the basket.

The winch operator saw what was happening and increased the speed of the winch, drawing the cable and basket up at a faster rate. Ethan didn't stop shimmying up the cable. He needed every inch he could get so as to be above the beast when it hit. He turned to look at it without stopping his upward motion. He had to know where it was. Maybe it would pass below the entire basket rig and splash back into the sea?

But this hope was dashed as soon as Ethan eyeballed the Jurassic reptile. The aquatic behemoth's mandibles snapped around both ends of the basket, a few of its six-inch teeth breaking off in the process. Ethan jerked both of his feet up, bending his legs sharply at the knees out of fear the monster aqua-beast would be able to reach his lower extremities and do away with them. He did not want to make it all the way into the helicopter only to be hauled aboard with a pair of bloody stumps dumping his blood over the ocean as they flew away.

What he should have been worried about was being knocked from the cable back into the ocean, for the raging *Liopleurodon* latched onto the steel bars of the cage and hung there. Its multi-tons of weight canting the helo to one side, tossing the winch operator out the open door. The man reached out as he plunged, swiping for the cable but missing. He fell head first until he reached Ethan, who reached out with his right arm—and right leg—in an attempt to break the airman's fall, or at least stall it enough to allow him to reach out and grab the cable.

The winch operator's helmet impacted Ethan's face, smashing his nose, releasing a gout of blood. The photographer shouted in pain, but hooked his elbow under the plummeting airman's armpit. Then he used his right leg to shove his would-be rescuer toward him on the cable. The winch man hugged Ethan until he was certain his fall had been arrested, then he grabbed onto the cable himself and began pulling himself up, hand over hand.

Ethan stared down at the *Liopleurodon*, noting with mounting terror that it was still hanging by its jaws from the cage, its long body writhing and wriggling. He shouted to the man whose life he had likely just saved.

"The cable's not moving—anybody else up there with you to flip it back on?"

The airman shook his head. "Just the pilot and he's got his hands full. I'll make it up, then I'll reel you in."

Ethan had his doubts about this, considering what had just happened, but he waited until the winch man was a few feet up the cable and then pulled himself up an arm's length at a time as well. As they neared the helicopter's undercarriage, the pilot could be heard bellowing choice expletives over the engine roar, no doubt related to the fact that the *Liopleurodon's* sheer weight threatened to pull the chopper down into the sea. Ethan stared wide-eyed as the surface of the ocean came closer and closer.

As more of the aquatic predator's body was dipped back into the ocean, its tail movements became much more powerful, now having the saltwater to push its muscles against. The basket started to swing and gyrate wildly, nearly knocking Ethan from the cable, shredding the skin on his hands. Seeing the airman hook an arm over the 'copter's door frame buoyed Ethan's spirits, though, and he doubled down on his own grip.

Pull up...come on, just pull up...now the other arm, pull...

He lapsed into a working trance, pulling himself arm over arm, entwining his legs around the cable to keep him from slipping down toward the *Liopleurodon*, which was threatening to take down the entire helicopter by its sheer weight.

The voice of the winch operator permeated Ethan's tunnel-vision thoughts. "Grab my hand! Grab it, I've got you, come on!"

Ethan hadn't realized how close he was. His eyes were open, but he hadn't really been seeing anything. Now he forced his brain to make sense of what his eyes could see. The airman's right hand, outstretched, beckoning, while his left was looped around a hand strap over the door frame.

Ethan reached up with his right hand and felt the winch operator's grip at the same time as the helicopter plummeted sharply downward. The airman yelled to the pilot. "Got him—up, up, up!"

Ethan felt himself being yanked aboard, where he slid across the cargo bay floor, coming to a stop facing the other door, also open.

"Drop the cable—drop it!" The pilot's frantic command galvanized the winch operator into action. He moved to the winch and unclipped the hook that fastened the basket cable to the spool. He tossed the cable out of the aircraft.

"Done!"

Ethan propped himself up on his elbows and stared down out of the open door in time to see the basket—with the *Liopleurodon* still clinging on by its stubborn jaws—splash back into the ocean. The pilot wrangled with the collective until the helicopter was stabilized, then gained altitude in a controlled fashion. Ethan looked about the mostly empty aircraft, at the mechanical restraints set into the floor, now empty, that had held the bombs that had unleashed so much destruction on the island.

He glanced at the pilot and the winch operator, surprised that only two persons had unleashed so much mayhem. He didn't recognize either of them; neither were part of the crew who had dropped the team off in the civilian helicopter, and neither wore military uniforms. Ethan rose unsteadily to his feet and moved to a jump seat next to the winch operator and sat down, gripping a hand strap to secure him in the event of turbulence.

The winch man looked at Ethan with a big grin. He wore mirrored aviator glasses, but looked Ethan in the eyes anyway. "Glad we saw your signal! Thirty more seconds and we'd have been long gone. You injured—anything that can't wait?"

Ethan shook his head, accepting a first-aid kit from the airman that he would use to clean up his bloody nose.

"Thank you."

The airman nodded, wrapping a blanket around Ethan and handing him a bottle of water and some food. "No, thank you, Mr., Jones. If it weren't for you..." He shook his head slowly while staring down into the ocean speeding by below. "We'll be in

American Samoa in about two hours. Sit back, relax and enjoy the flight." Then he joined the pilot up front in the cockpit, leaving Ethan to stare out the open door in silence.

The island was now not much more than a heap of smoldering lava, sending black smoke into the atmosphere. Ethan picked up his camera and aimed it at the devastation. He clicked off a shot as the island smoldered and crumbled into the sea from whence it came.

CHAPTER 36

Nuku'alofa, Tonga

CIA Special Agent Valea Esau sat on the bus with his teeth clenched as the king's palace passed outside the window. All around him people sat and stood, some with small cages containing live chickens or roosters, some with bundles of whole fish. All chatted loudly, going about their day bringing goods to and from the markets with a comfortable routine that Esau envied. He could no longer really remember what it was like to have such a normal life, for he'd given his up to The Company long ago. His was a world of lies, dark networks, subterfuge, and a constant undercurrent of danger. And for what? To supposedly support a country he no longer even lived in, may never live in again for all he knew.

Maybe I've been in the tropics for too long, he mused, watching the palace grounds whiz by outside. His stop would be three more past, so as not to be seen directly taking the bus to the palace. A walk of about a mile, but he was used to such inconveniences in the line of duty. They reached the first stop after the palace, and his gaze traveled reflexively to the bus doors as a new gaggle of riders got on. He watched them from behind his sunglasses, checking to see if any were scanning the people in the seats, beyond the normal *where should I sit* glances. None of them seemed to be anything other than what they appeared, but nevertheless, his fingers clutched down tighter on the object beside him in the seat.

It looked like an ordinary mechanic's ratchet set case, with a well-known tool maker's logo in raised plastic lettering on the side. It fit in perfectly with the grease-stained jumpsuit he wore with the local auto mechanic shop logo sewn on the breast pocket. But inside the case, one would not find the ordinary compliment of tools. In fact, the molded plastic inlays that were form-fitted to the tools they were supposed to hold had been removed altogether. This had been done by Valea himself in order to create more room inside the case for what he needed to carry inconspicuously: cash. One million dollars' worth of U.S. bills, non-sequential and unmarked. Meant for the Tongan king as an under-the-table token payment for the failed Neptune's Inferno attempt at creating a permanent new island on which a U.S. military installation could be supported in return for a revenue stream, Valea was meeting with the king today to give him this payment.

He passed the second bus stop after the palace and looked around the bus again. No suspicious activity. He gave himself the all-clear to exit the bus at the next stop, after a visual check of that area from inside the bus, of course. He looked down at the tool case, eyeballing the clasps, making sure they were secured for the hundredth time. *It's a go,* he told himself, but as the bus churned on toward the third stop after the palace, he wasn't feeling it. He ran his fingers over the case, his eyes seeing the bundles of greenbacks inside as though he had X-ray vision.

Was he really going to give all this money to a king? Literally, a king, someone whose life would not change a whit if he didn't receive it. Whereas Valea himself, what did he have to look forward to without this money? Fifteen more years of government service, risking his life? The thought coalesced rapidly, forming itself from previous notions waiting to be assembled together. By the time the bus reached Valea's planned stop, the thought had formed into a full-fledged plan.

To hell with it. I'm done, I don't need this. As a covert agent, technically a spy in the way most people thought of the term, Valea knew how to disappear. Even with the relatively meager resources he already had at his disposal, he could probably do it. But with an extra million in untraceable cash? He'd be set. Sure, the CIA will look for him, he had no doubts about that. He'd never be able to safely return to the U.S. or the South Pacific, but it's not like he killed one of their own or something that would trigger a no-holds-barred international manhunt. They wouldn't look too hard, especially if he stayed out of trouble, which he planned to. A low-key existence in some hospitable climate far removed from the intel community was just what he needed. *South America?* He'd think of something.

Contrary to what he might have expected, once he had resolved himself to this new course of action, to this new life, he became more relaxed, less nervous. That didn't mean he would drop his situational awareness. He would never be able to afford to do that. But as he stared at a map of routes on a placard at the front of the bus, he knew where he was going right now.

Valea remained seated as the bus came to a halt for the third stop after the palace. Outside the window, he saw nothing out of the ordinary that would have prevented him from making his planned exit. He pictured Malo's face, his reaction when he would give him the money, the shots of liquor he'd have lined up for them once he turned it over. *Sorry, Your Majesty, your drinks are good but they're not that good. Not a million bucks good.*

The bus started up again and left the third stop behind. Valea clutched his tool case and smiled. A new island had risen from the sea, and with it, a pile of cash. Soon that island would be blasted back into the sea, and the money, too, would retreat.

With Valea.

EPILOGUE

Washington, D.C., The White House Situation Room

President Linda Mallory addressed the dozen or so people seated around the table. None of them looked particularly happy, including herself. "So, this was taken when?"

She nodded to a photo on a large wall monitor of *Hunga Tonga-Ha'apai* sinking beneath the waves in a fiery, hell-born fury. Even with no manmade elements in the photo, it depicted a scene of chaotic destruction.

James Elkweather, a mid-career CIA analyst, responded from behind thick spectacles. "This was taken about twelve hours ago by the lone surviving member of U.N. Expedition Gaia, Australian wildlife photographer Ethan Jones."

The president reflected a moment longer as she stared at the hypnotic image. "So the planet's newest land is no longer." She shook her head slowly, as if she couldn't believe it, or was perhaps contemplating the significance of it.

Elkweather nodded. "That is correct, Madam President. The seamount—that's an undersea mountain—is closer to the surface now than it was before the...eruption...but it will always remain permanently submerged."

The president's face took on a stern look as she addressed those in attendance. "I was told that the goal of Neptune's Inferno was to deliberately trigger earthquakes that would, in turn, result in desirable chain reactions—such as directed tsunamis, volcanoes that form new land—not prehistoric animals." She ended by glaring at the scientist responsible for spearheading the ultra-secret project. That man, Hungarian-American János Gombos, shrugged before meeting her gaze with a level stare.

"Call the dinosaurs an unintended side-effect. As you know, the purpose of the program was to create a new island that might be used as a strategic base by the U.S. and its allies in the region. We were never one hundred percent sure on how exactly that might take shape. That is why we had a spy in the expedition, to keep us apprised of unintended consequences and to stack the deck in our favor in case things did not go our way, which they didn't."

The president's eyes flicked to her laptop screen for a moment. "Richard Eavesley, the British explorer?"

Elkweather, the analyst, nodded. "He was our mole."

"Do we know what happened to him? Is it certain he's dead, is what I'm asking, because if this ever gets out…"

"He's dead. Mr. Jones said he was eaten by a hadrosaur."

"What's that?" the president asked.

Elkweather nodded to an assistant who cycled through some images on a laptop PowerPoint and then displayed one on the wall monitor. It depicted a large four-legged dinosaur (with silhouette figure of an adult human male for comparison), with a fleshy waddle on its head. Most of those around the table grimaced or looked away as they imagined how terrible Eavesley's fate must have been.

Elkweather continued. "If we're lucky, he even has video of it. They're all dead except for Jones and the helicopter crews who brought the expedition in and out, that is confirmed. The entire Tongan landing party who got there first were confirmed perished by the U.N. team, as well."

A moment of silent reflection ensued during which everyone seemed to breathe a sigh of relief. Until it was broken by an aide for the Secretary of State. "Unfortunately, Madam President, Richard Eavesley is not the worst of our problems with respect to leaking details of Neptune's Inferno."

The president glared at the middle-aged, balding man who had delivered this unpleasant news. "Explain yourself."

"The State Department has received official word from Tonga—from King Malo himself—that the United States has not kept its word on a deal regarding the formation of a new island. He's threatening to go public if he doesn't receive a one million dollar cash payment that he says was promised to him directly by

CIA operative, Valea Esau. Esau was our field agent based in Tonga, attached to our embassy in Fiji."

"And what does Agent Esau have to say about this? I presume you've been in contact with him?"

The aide looked uncomfortable, but proceeded. "In fact, Madam President, we have been unable to reach Agent Esau after numerous attempts to contact him. He appears to be missing in action. Additional agents are being dispatched to Tonga now to look for him."

The president nodded and then waved a hand dismissively. "All right. Pay Tonga the million, right away."

The aide nodded, making a note on a pad. "In the meantime, we'll track down the money that we gave—"

"Do it *now!*" the president yelled. "We don't need this to become an international incident. Pay the man."

The aide nodded again and left the room. The president turned back to those still seated at the table. "Anybody else have anything pressing that I should know about?"

No one said anything. The president went on. "What about the dinosaurs, then, are they a threat? Can they reach other, populated islands? I'm not going to wake up tomorrow to headlines about *T. rex*es chomping tourists on the beaches of Tahiti or somewhere, am I? Hell, I'm *going* to Tahiti this winter, right?" She turned to an assistant who consulted a schedule on a smartphone before nodding.

Another man answered, one of the scientists on Neptune's Inferno, Dr. Marcus Ollenstein, a marine geophysics expert. "Most of the dinosaurs surely perished in the bombing, but it is possible that a few individuals escaped. However, we think it unlikely that two or more breeding individuals could have made it, so when the lone stragglers die off due to natural causes, that should be it for those evolutionary throwbacks."

The president looked away from Ethan's photo at her expectant group. "Overall, would you say the technology utilized in Neptune's Inferno was successful? It *will* trigger earthquakes, generate tsunamis on demand…?"

János Gombos nodded convincingly. "Absolutely."

The president's gaze returned to Ethan's image. "Wait a year and try again somewhere else."

THE END

SEVEREDPRESS

f facebook.com/severedpress

twitter.com/severedpress

CHECK OUT OTHER GREAT
DINOSAUR THRILLERS

JURASSIC ISLAND
by Viktor Zarkov

Guided by satellite photos and modern technology a ragtag group of survivalists and scientists travel to an uncharted island in the remote South Indian Ocean. Things go to hell in a hurry once the team reaches the island and the massive megalodon that attacked their boats is only the beginning of their desperate fight for survival.

Nothing could have prepared billionaire explorer Joseph Thornton and washed up archaeologist Christopher "Colt" McKinnon for the terrifying prehistoric creatures that wait for them on JURASSIC ISLAND!

K-REX
by L.Z. Hunter

Deep within the Congo jungle, Circuitz Mining employs mercenaries as security for its Coltan mining site. Armed with assault rifles and decades of experience, nothing should go wrong. However, the dangers within the jungle stretch beyond venomous snakes and poisonous spiders. There is more to fear than guerrillas and vicious animals. Undetected, something lurks under the expansive treetop canopy...

Something ancient.

Something dangerous.

Kasai Rex!

CHECK OUT OTHER GREAT DINOSAUR THRILLERS

SPINOSAURUS
by Hugo Navikov

Brett Russell is a hunter of the rarest game. His targets are cryptids, animals denied by science. But they are well known by those living on the edges of civilization, where monsters attack and devour their animals and children and lay ruin to their shantytowns.

When a shadowy organization sends Brett to the Congo in search of the legendary dinosaur cryptid Kasai Rex, he will face much more than a terrifying monster from the past.

Spinosaurus is a dinosaur thriller packed with intrigue, action and giant prehistoric predators.

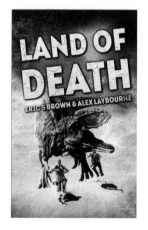

LAND OF DEATH
by Eric S Brown & Alex Laybourne

A group of American soldiers, fleeing an organized attack on their base camp in the Middle East, encounter a storm unlike anything they've seen before. When the storm subsides, they wake up to find themselves no longer in the desert and perhaps not even on Earth. The jungle they've been deposited in is a place ruled by prehistoric creatures long extinct. Each day is a struggle to survive as their ammo begins to run low and virtually everything they encounter, in this land they've been hurled into, is a deadly threat.

SEVERED**PRESS**

f facebook.com/severedpress

twitter.com/severedpress

CHECK OUT OTHER GREAT DINOSAUR THRILLERS

WRITTEN IN STONE
by David Rhodes

Charles Dawson is trapped 100 million years in the past. Trying to survive from day to day in a world of dinosaurs he devises a plan to change his fate. As he begins to write messages in the soft mud of a nearby stream, he can only hope they will be found by someone who can stop his time travel. Professor Ron Fontana and Professor Ray Taggit, scientists with opposing views, each discover the fossilized messages. While attempting to save Charles, Professor Fontana, his daughter Lauren and their friend Danny are forced to join Taggit and his group of mercenaries. Taggit does not intend to rescue Charles Dawson, but to force Dawson to travel back in time to gather samples for Taggit's fame and fortune. As the two groups jump through time they find they must work together to make it back alive as this fast-paced thriller climaxes at the very moment the age of dinosaurs is ending.

HARD TIME
by Alex Laybourne

Rookie officer Peter Malone and his heavily armed team are sent on a deadly mission to extract a dangerous criminal from a classified prison world. A Kruger Correctional facility where only the hardest, most vicious criminals are sent to fend for themselves, never to return.

But when the team come face to face with ancient beasts from a lost world, their mission is changed. The new objective: Survive.

CHECK OUT OTHER GREAT
DINOSAUR THRILLERS

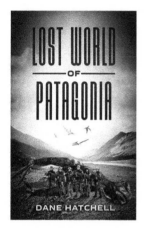

LOST WORLD OF PATAGONIA
by Dane Hatchell

An earthquake opens a path to a land hidden for millions of years. Under the guise of finding cryptid animals, Ace Corporation sends Alex Klasse, a Cryptozoologist and university professor, his associates, and a band of mercenaries to explore the Lost World of Patagonia. The crew boards a nuclear powered All-Terrain Tracked Carrier and takes a harrowing ride into the unknown.

The expedition soon discovers prehistoric creatures still exist. But the dangers won't prevent a sub-team from leaving the group in search of rare jewels. Tensions run high as personalities clash, and man proves to be just as deadly as the dinosaurs that roam the countryside.

Lost World of Patagonia is a prehistoric thriller filled with murder, mayhem, and savage dinosaur action.

SAVAGE ISLAND
by Alan Spencer

Somewhere in the Atlantic Ocean, an uncharted island has been used for the illegal dumping of chemicals and pollutants for years by Globo Corp's. Private investigator Pierce Range will learn plenty about the evil conglomerate when Susan Branch, an environmentalist from The Green Project, hires him to join the expedition to save her kidnapped father from Globo Corp's evil hands.

Things go to hell in a hurry once the team reaches the island. The bloodthirsty dinosaurs and voracious cannibals are only the beginning of the fight for survival. Pierce must unlock the mysteries surrounding the toxic operation and somehow remain in one piece to complete the rescue mission.

Ratchet up the body count, because this mission will leave the killing floor soaked in blood and chewed up corpses. When the insane battle ends, will there by anybody left alive to survive Savage Island?

CPSIA information can be obtained
at www.ICGtesting.com
Printed in the USA
LVHW021547180419
614686LV00005B/853